Best Friends Forever

D0101355

Best Friends Forever

Holly & Kelly Willoughby

Orion
Children's Books

First published in Great Britain in 2016 by Hodder and Stoughton

1 3 5 7 9 10 8 6 4 2

Text © Holly Willoughby and Kelly Willoughby, 2016

The moral rights of the authors have been asserted.

A CIP catalogue record for this book is available from the British Library.

ISBN 978 1 4440 1461 7

Printed and bound in Great Britain by Clays Ltd, St Ives plc

The paper and board used in this book are made
from wood from responsible sources.

It's never too late to say you're sorry
and open the door on friendship. No matter
how bad it's been and how tough the road ahead
might be, give it a go. Life is too short for regrets.

Contents

1   Back to L'Etoile

2   The Piggle Effect

3   Unexpected Announcement

4   So Much to Discuss!

5   A Lesson in Positivity

6   An Unfair Advantage

7   France, Here We Come!

8   Chateau Pierre

9   WATC

10   *La Grande Expedition:* Day One

11   Crossing A Line

12   The Leopard Who Changed Her Spots

13   How to Outfox the Fox!

14 *La Grande Expedition:* Day Two

15 A Really Bad Feeling Saves The Day

16 *Table Vert*

17 Crossing The Finish Line

18 Home At Last

19 Christmas Countdown

Welcome back, Story-seeker, to another term at L'Etoile, School for Stars,

You join our girls at one of the most exciting times of their school lives. They're about to embark on their first overseas school trip . . . at least, it should be exciting, but some of our more pampered Etoilettes aren't particularly thrilled by the prospect of camping in the big outdoors. But determined, as ever, to get the best from every situation, they roll up their sleeves and throw themselves into Madame Ruby's orienteering extravaganza. It won't come as any surprise to you seasoned Etoilettes that things don't quite go as expected, and nothing could prepare the girls for what awaits them en France.

Grab your hiking boots, everyone, and fasten your seatbelts for another twisting and turning School for Stars adventure.

Bon chance, L'Etoilettes, bon chance!

Love,
Holly & Kelly Willoughby x

1

Back to L'Etoile

'Can you believe we're fourth-years?' Molly Fitzfoster said to her twin sister Maria as she leapt out of their dad's old Bentley onto the L'Etoile driveway.

'I know!' Maria said. 'Where did the time go? I can still remember the first time we stood on this gravel, looking up at that big gold star and wondering what was waiting for us on the other side of those doors. It's so weird to think we've got more time behind us now than we have left at L'Etoile.'

'Well, don't go wishing our last years away before we've even begun this one!' Sally said, having collected her suitcase from the ever-obliging Eddie, the Fitzfoster family driver.

Beep, beep!

'Who's that?' Molly said, hearing her sister's mobile signal that she had a text.

'Wow, I've missed three messages while we've been chatting in the car,' Maria said. 'One from Dad, saying his driver collected Pippa from London this morning and they are fifteen minutes away – but that was about thirteen minutes ago so she'll be here any moment; one from Mum, reminding us to phone home more this term . . . we must try and do that, Moll; and one from Princess Ameera, saying she's just bought a wall calendar so she can tick the days off until she flies over in December to see us!'

'I still can't believe she's coming!' Molly blushed. She was secretly still a little overwhelmed by the fact that she had a real life princess on speed-dial.

If you remember, Story-seeker, Princess Ameera, an Indian princess, joined L'Etoile at the start of last term to experience life at a British school and immediately became one of the girls' closest friends, much to Molly and her friend Honey's dreamy delight!

'How sweet is that?' Molly added, trying to play it a bit cooler. 'It's such a shame she couldn't come back this term as a full-time student. She was totally one of us!' Molly was also remembering the princess's extensive, OOTW wardrobe.

OOTW = Out of this world, Story-seeker.

'I know, but I think things are going to be so much better for her in India now,' Maria said. 'There'll be a lot of public support and she'll have more freedom to become the person she really wants to be.'

'I hope so,' Sally said, missing her royal friend immensely. Sally had been blown away when Madame Ruby entrusted her to look after the princess when she'd arrived at L'Etoile. She'd helped Ameera settle in by showing her around and introducing her to all the girls, and in return, Ameera had done wonders for Sally's self-confidence.

'December's not far away, Sal. You know how quickly the term zips by. We'll be on our way to meet Ameera at that Chelsea match Dad got us all tickets for before you know it,' Maria said.

'Look!' Molly cried with excitement. 'Here come the twins!'

By the girls, Story-seeker, Molly means the other set of twins in their year, Danya and Honey Sawyer, who, after a bumpy introduction, have become as close to them as their existing BFFs, Sally and Pippa.

The girls hadn't seen as much of Danya and Honey as they usually did over the summer, because their families had holidayed abroad this year, so they were all busting to catch up.

'Molly! Hi!' Honey cried, diving out of the car almost before it had stopped.

'Maria! Molly!' Danya called from behind.

'Oooooh, we've missed you!' Molly squealed. 'I can't believe you guys couldn't make it down to Wilton House this summer. We had a blast, didn't we, Sal?'

Sally nodded, thinking how much her life had changed since her mum had started working for the Fitzfosters in their house in the country. They were both treated like members of the family and, for the first time in her life, Sally knew what it must feel like to have sisters.

'Tell us about it! Mum and Dad got it into their heads that a family road trip across Route 66 in America was a brilliant plan – which it would have been if baby Flori hadn't teethed her way across the country!' Danya said with a yawn.

'Ah, poor thing. How's she doing?' Molly said. She loved babies and had secretly been quite envious when Flori had arrived in the Easter holidays. She would have loved a little sister to dress up and play with.

'She's so cute! Look!' Honey said, scrolling through the gorgeous smiley baby photos she'd taken of Flori that summer.

'Adorable! Your mum HAS to bring her when they come to collect you guys at the end of term,' Molly cooed. 'Promise!'

'Definitely!' Danya said.

'YO!' a voice shouted from behind.

'Pippa!' Sally said, swinging around to hug her.

'Ah, Sally. You'd think we hadn't seen each other all summer. I only said goodbye yesterday! What a welcome,' Pippa grinned, putting her suitcase down for a proper hug.

'I know – I know, but you're my *almost* twin – you know that! There are three sets in this group of ours!' Sally said, giggling.

'Happy to hear it!' Pippa said, who had also grown up without any brothers or sisters.

'Watch out, guys! Here comes the seventh member

of the family!' Maria said suddenly, as she spied L'Etoile's guard dog and their very best four-legged friend bounding towards them.

'Twinkle-toes!' Molly cried, though her expression quickly changed as Twinkle got closer and she saw that the little dog was covered in mud.

'Twinkle . . . noooo!!!!!' Molly screamed, but it was too late. Twinkle had already leapt into her arms and was wriggling about gleefully, smearing every inch of her in brown sludge.

Molly was momentarily shocked into silence, before she realised it was too late to scold Twinkle now.

(Not to mention the perfect excuse for an outfit change, Story-seeker.)

'Oh, whatever!' she said. 'Too late to worry about my brand new *Look Like a Star* winter coat! Thank goodness it's not *dry clean only!*'

The sight of the usually pristine Molly Fitzfoster, looking as though she'd been dragged through a mud bath, was just too funny for anyone to keep a straight face and everyone on the drive was laughing their heads off.

'Oh, really?' Molly said, sensing she had become

the first joke of the term. 'It's like that, is it?' A wicked thought crossed her mind and she put the little dog down in the middle of the friendship circle.

'Twinkle, darling. You're still wet! Why don't you shake it off?' she suggested, and Twinkle, who had an almost human knack for understanding exactly what you said to her, shook with all her might, showering the girls with muddy droplets.

'Twink-le!' the others shouted.

'Ha! Now that's funny!' Molly said with a grin.

'Twinkle! You naughty dog!' a gruff voice said. The burly caretaker, Mr Hart, appeared. He took one look at the girls and one look at his beloved dog (whom the girls had, of course, given the most girly name possible) and his face fell.

'Oh, don't worry, Mr Hart. Had it been anyone but Twinkle, Molly would have phoned the police by now!' Maria grinned, wiping dirty water off her cheek.

'I'm so sorry, girls. I was on my way to Garland to change some of the light bulbs, when Twinkle spied a rabbit in the quad and before I had chance to get hold of her, she took the quickest route through the water-logged vegetable patch to try and catch up with it,' Mr Hart said, embarrassed, but equally amused at the sight of his favourite L'Etoile students covered in mud.

'It's worth it just to see her lovely face after all this time,' Honey said, fondling Twinkle's ears.

'You'd best get yourselves to Garland and change before supper, and don't leave a muddy mess in the bathroom. Miss Coates is particularly highly strung this morning, since half the bedding didn't arrive back from the cleaners,' Mr Hart said.

'Right you are,' Danya said. 'And thanks for the warning.'

'Yes, thanks, Mr H!' Maria said. 'Great to see you looking so well!'

'Thank you, Maria!' Mr Hart said. He was feeling the happiest he'd felt for a long time. He had a secret he wanted to shout from the rooftops, but he knew he had to hold onto it for just a little bit longer.

2

The Piggle Effect

As the girls unpacked their things into their old room, which had an adjoining door to the Sawyer twins', they chatted about what fun they'd had over the summer and all the things they had to look forward to in the run up to Christmas.

'I can't believe your première is so soon, Moll!' Honey said, having emptied her suitcases in record time. She was sitting on Molly's bed showing her a pair of gorgeous new skinny jeans her mum had bought her in America.

'I know! I need to find something to wear – and while those jeans are simply TDF! I don't think

they're dressy enough for the red carpet, do you?'
Molly said.

TOF = To Die For. Story-seeker.

'Of course they're not!' Honey cried. 'I can't believe
you're even considering it!'

Molly giggled. 'Just kidding! Of course I can't
wear jeans to a Leicester Square film première! And
neither can you!'

'What?!' Honey said.

'I said, and neither can you, so you'd best get on the
Internet and order yourself something befitting a red
carpet event!' Molly said, her eyes twinkling.

'Are you saying what I think you're saying?' Honey
said, scarcely daring to breathe. Was her best friend
really telling her she had an invitation to the première
of the decade?

'Yep!' Molly exploded. 'In fact, listen up everyone!
You're all invited!'

Danya's head appeared at the adjoining door, the code
for which she'd secretly hacked so they could lock and
unlock it at will, without Miss Coates ever knowing.

'That's so exciting! Are you sure we're allowed to
come?' Danya asked.

'Exciting?' Honey, Sally and Pippa shouted. 'It's OOTW!'

OOTW = Out of this world, Story-seeker.

'Oh, my goodness. Now I feel like I'm in a movie!' Honey said.

'Ah, I love a good reaction,' Molly said. 'And that was great!'

'How did you manage it? Surely getting our names on that guest list was like trying to make a reservation at Buckingham Palace for Christmas lunch!' Pippa said.

'I'm not sure, if I'm honest,' Molly said. 'I think Dad might have pulled a few strings. One of the top guys at Warner Brothers contacted him to source a rare pink diamond ring so he could propose to his girlfriend and as soon as I saw the paperwork on the kitchen table, I knew we could use it to our advantage. All the other actors have only been allowed a plus *one*. And *I* now have a plus *five*!'

'Cooool!' Sally said dreamily.

'What a brilliant start to the term,' Honey said, lying back on Molly's bed, imagining herself swooshing down a long red carpet, to the flashing of photographers' cameras.

'I know, right?' Molly said. 'But I'm not the only one with OOTW news, am I, Pippa Burrows?'

Pippa blushed. 'Erm, yes. Well, you know One Direction liked one of the songs I co-wrote with Uncle Harry?'

'Yes!' the others shouted.

'They've decided to release it as their Christmas single!'

'No way!' Danya said.

Maria grinned in surprise at Danya's reaction. Who knew the cool, calm Danya Sawyer would go weak at the knees for a *boy band*?

'Yes way!' Pippa said proudly. 'And . . .'

'There's an 'and'?' Sally squealed. 'I can't believe you didn't tell me any of this!'

Pippa shot Sally an I'm-sorry-but-I-was-sworn-to-secrecy look.

'And . . . the reason I left Wilton House early yesterday is because they want MY backing vocals on the track. I went straight to the studios to meet them and record!' Pippa said. She was almost teary with excitement.

'I'm so jealous right now, I can't even look at you!' Danya said.

'Ditto!' Molly and Honey exclaimed.

'Tell me you've got a million selfies on your phone with the boys!' Danya said.

'I went one better than that!' Pippa grinned as she handed Maria a blue memory stick.

Maria stuck it into the side of her laptop as the others gathered around.

'Hi, Sally, Maria, Molly, Danya, Honey. We're One Direction. A little, extraordinarily talented, birdy told us you're our biggest fans so we thought we'd dedicate this Christmas single to you guys, Pippa's BFFs. Hope you enjoy it!'

Everyone in the room watched in stunned silence as the video of the boys recording Pippa's song, with Pippa, played.

Christmas-time for you and for me
Christmas-time for family
And if you don't know where to go
Meet me under the mistletoe

'Well?' Pippa said, as the final sleigh bells faded to silence.

It was safe to say that her friends were dumbfounded.

'Danya! Molly! Say something!' Pippa said. She was starting to worry they hadn't liked the song.

'Pippa Burrows. You have just hit the big time!' Maria said, having gathered her thoughts. She wasn't the biggest One Direction fan, but even she could appreciate that what she'd just witnessed was absolutely sensational.

'I actually think that might be my most favourite of all your songs. I'm so proud of you!' Sally said.

'Ditto!' Honey said.

'Me too!' Molly said. 'You've eclipsed my feature film with a two-minute song. You're a genius!'

'Oh, I love you, girls,' Pippa said, glowing.

Suddenly everyone looked at Danya, aware she hadn't passed her usual judgment on the situation.

'I'll meet them under the mistletoe,' Danya said dreamily.

'Dan!' Honey said. 'A little bit of focus, please? Pips wants some feedback!'

'I, errr . . . I feel like I can't comment thoroughly until I watch it a few more times. Would that be OK? And can you pause on the bit where Harry Styles says my name and looks at me?' Danya said.

'Looks at you?' Pippa giggled. 'Danya, you're hilarious.'

'Just play it!' Danya said.

'I think you'd better put it on repeat and then make Dan her own copy or she's going to drive you crazy!' Honey grinned.

'Heaven help us!' Maria said, rolling her eyes.

'I'm just glad you like it!' Pippa said. 'Dan, you can hold onto that copy. I have a few more memory sticks in my bag. Just in case . . . you know!'

And so it began. The girls settled into their usual first night back at school routine of a midnight feast and gossip and, boy, did they have a lot to talk about!

3

Unexpected Announcement

'Where's Danya?' Maria whispered to Honey as they filed into the corridor the following morning.

'Will you get her, Maria?' Honey said. 'She'll listen to you. She must have watched that flipping 1D video ten thousand times since last night! I swear she's gone mad!'

'Hilarious!' Maria said. 'Leave it with me. I'll bring her back to reality!'

Five minutes later, all six girls were sat cross-legged on the floor of the Kodak Hall, awaiting the arrival of their headmistress, Madame Ruby, for one of her legendary first assemblies of the term. It was customary during these assemblies for the girls to find out what awaited them that term and they'd come to look forward to seeing Madame Ruby bubbling with excitement over whatever it was she had planned for them.

'Shhh . . . here she comes!' Pippa whispered as they heard the familiar swooshing of the headmistress's skirts across the stage.

'Welcome back, L'Etoilettes, to this, the first day of a new school year,' Madame Ruby began, a vision in purple silk and her trademark ruby red lipstick. 'As ever, I trust you had a wonderful summer and that you are returned with the fervour and tenacity required to make this term your best yet!'

Muffled enthusiasm pulsed around the room.

'I don't usually start these gatherings by telling you what I've been up to during the holidays, but seeing where my vacation has led us, that is where I'll begin . . .'

'This sounds ominous!' Maria whispered to Danya, whose feet she'd managed to drag firmly back onto L'Etoile soil.

'I can't even begin to imagine!' Danya answered.

'France!' Madame Ruby said simply.

'What?' Maria exclaimed. Of all the words she'd

been expecting to come out of the headmistress's mouth, *France* wasn't one of them!

'Actually, the south of France, to be precise,' Madame Ruby said in Maria's direction, as though she'd heard her. She always had a knack of making every student in the room feel as though her full attention were on her and her alone.

'I have just spent the most wonderful of summers with a dear friend of mine, at her chateau, situated in the mountains above Nice, in the Parc du Mercantour. The views are breath-taking, with the peaks of the Southern Alps behind and the Mediterranean stretching away in front.' Madame Ruby stopped, as if she were imagining herself back on that mountainside, gazing into the distance.

'Now seaside-Nice I could handle, but I'm not sure about mountainous-Nice!' Honey whispered, recalling a glamorous family holiday they'd spent on the glitzy Cote d'Azur.

The headmistress continued. 'Madame Pierre and her family run an outdoorsy team-building programme for students like yourselves; a sort of mini expedition, and from what I saw during the summer, you are going to love it, L'Etoilettes!'

Contrary to the ripple of excitement which usually

travelled around the Kodak Hall following one of Madame Ruby's announcements, today it was so quiet you could have heard a pin drop. The expressions on Molly and Honey's faces said it all.

'Ex-ped-ition!' they mouthed at each other in horror.

'I bet *she* didn't trek up too many mountains while she was there!' Pippa said to Danya.

Aware she had sent her audience into somewhat of a tailspin, given the absence of any singing or dancing in her announcement, Madame Ruby attempted to explain further.

'To succeed in life, L'Etoilettes, you not only need to harness and exceed your own potential, but to realise the potential you can achieve when you work as a group. I'm talking about team work, L'Etoilettes, team work!' She paused, then, seeing several students nodding in agreement, continued.

'The Pierre family have hit upon a terrific idea which will give each of you the opportunity to connect with the great outdoors and hone new skills you simply wouldn't get the chance to develop here at L'Etoile. You will form teams of no more than six and each year group will travel to France to take part in their own weekend-long expedition. You will, of course, receive instruction on the basics of orienteering before you embark on your trip, but the name of the game here is to work together – combining your individual skills to ensure your success. There is no 'I' in 'team', L'Etoilettes!'

'No, but there's a "me" in "team"!' Honey muttered, wondering how she was going to cope without a socket for her hair straighteners.

'But it's autumn! Soon to be winter! It will be freeeeezing!' Molly whispered to Maria in alarm. 'I'm sure mountaineering in the Alps is delightful in August, but not when it's snowing! I can't bear it!'

Madame Ruby held up her hand.

'I know you all have a hundred questions, and these will be addressed by your form tutors in the next couple of hours. For now, I just have one thing to add on this subject and that is that you won't be alone at the chateau . . .'

'Wolves!' Sally gasped, just loud enough to be heard, much to her mortification.

'No. Not wolves!' Madame Ruby replied. 'You will be in competition with other schools, so please remember that as soon as you leave here, you are ambassadors for L'Etoile and you should behave in a way that would make me and your school proud.'

She paused again as an applause went round. The students seemed to be warming to the idea!

'On, then, to other, perhaps more L'Etoile-esque business. We are very honoured and proud to have among us two students who are about to fly the L'Etoile flag on the world's stage and to celebrate this, *OK!* Magazine will be coming to cover our school's end of term Christmas celebrations.'

'Now she's hotting up!' Lara Walters whispered to Belle Baldwin. 'Thank heavens for that!'

Molly's cheeks were on fire. Could Madame Ruby really be referring to her and Pippa? Surely not. Surely her mum would have said something to her if she'd had to give permission for her to appear in a magazine like *OK!*

'Molly Fitzfoster and Pippa Burrows, where are you, girls?' Madame Ruby said, scanning the room until her gaze fell upon them. 'Ah yes. Would you stand up, please?'

Both girls glowed with pride and embarrassment.

Madame Ruby explained. 'Molly has her first film première in London on the 19th December for the new Warner Brothers movie, which I know I've mentioned before . . . but, Molly, I want to wish you all the best. I'm sure the film will be a box office triumph.

We are all so incredibly proud of you. Well done, my dear.'

The room erupted with cheers.

'Woooohoooo!' Maria whooped.

'And, Pippa, and this will come as a huge surprise to most of you, has had one of her songs selected by the biggest boy band in the world, One Direction, to be their new Christmas single!'

Gasps, then more whooping and cheering followed.

'Not only that, I had it confirmed by Mr Fuller of Universal Records this morning that Pippa's own backing vocal was recorded for the track yesterday. Well done, Pippa. What an extraordinary achievement for such a young girl. We are immensely proud of you too!'

Every student in the room jumped up with excitement, and any that were sitting close enough to touch Pippa, did so, just in case it would bring them closer to their idols.

Pippa and Molly hugged each other until the applause had subsided.

'Taking these ladies' achievements into consideration, and the fact that you won't all have the usual time to prepare a huge Christmas *extravaganza*, the staff and I thought it might be lovely to have a traditional candlelit carol service this year. Each year group will nominate someone to do a reading or a musical solo, but the main event will be the fourth-year choir, given that the focus of *OK!* Magazine will be to get shots of both Pippa and Molly in action. Pippa, we wondered whether you could put together a special arrangement of the One Direction song for your classmates to perform? What do you think?'

Pippa barely had time to blush again, before the school went wild.

About eighty per cent of the assembly hall would be lying if they said they weren't secretly hoping for a surprise appearance by the band during the song, Story-seeker. Staff and students alike!

'And two more pieces of news a little closer to home. Firstly, the wonderful news that the lovely Mrs Fuller is expecting her first baby . . .'

Once again the room exploded into applause and cheers.

'So that's why Mr Hart looked so happy yesterday! He must have been bursting to tell us he's about to become a granddad,' Maria said to Molly.

'OMG, that's so cool!' Molly answered.

'She'll make the best mum!' Pippa said.

'Hurray! Hurrah!'

Mrs Fuller, whose cheeks were almost the colour of Pippa's – but not quite – gave a wave from her seat and a nod of thanks.

'With this in mind, please do your best to keep her stress levels to a minimum this term!' Madame Ruby continued, with a rare wink, which Maria could have sworn was specifically aimed at her.

'And finally . . .'

'What on earth can she possibly come out with next?' Alice Parks whispered to Honey.

'Some news regarding . . . well, me, actually . . .'

'No way – she's not going to say she's preggers too, is she?!' Sally giggled.

'This term will, in fact, be my last term at L'Etoile as your headmistress.' She paused as a gasp went up.

'What?! L'Etoile won't survive without her!' Maria exclaimed not as quietly as she might have.

'Yes, my L'Etoilettes. The time has come for me to hang up my ballet pointes, you might say, and pass the conductor's baton to someone else in the New Year. Naturally, it will come as no surprise that my permanent successor will eventually be Mrs Fuller, but until she returns from maternity leave at the end of next year, Mr Potts will take the helm.'

'Mr Potts?!'

'Has she lost her mind?'

The whole school was confused.

'Mr Potts has been with me at L'Etoile since the very beginning and knows it as well, if not better, than I do . . .'

'Doesn't make him capable of running the place, though!' Maria said to Danya.

'Yes – but just think of the fun we can have! We run rings around him in music, and with old Ruby and Fuller out of the picture, I'd say the New Year is shaping up swimmingly, wouldn't you, Maria?' Danya said with a wicked glint in her eye.

'Oh!' Maria said, her face cracking a cheeky smile. 'I see what you mean!'

'Mr Potts will make a superb leader for you all and I ask that you give him the same kind of support and respect you have shown me over the years,' Madame Ruby said, nodding in his direction. 'He will need every one of you behind him to take L'Etoile to new heights.'

Mr Potts shifted slightly uncomfortably in his seat.

'This is going to be a blast!' Danya said.

'On that note then, L'Etoilettes, I'll leave you in

the capable hands of your form tutors to discuss everything further. Have a super term, one and all, and *bon chance dans les Alpes*!' Madame Ruby said and swooshed off the stage.

4

So Much To Discuss!

'Settle down, girls, settle down, please,' called Miss Denham.

Molly and Honey were over the moon to discover that their new form tutor was to be their beloved drama teacher. Miss Denham had taught them drama every year since they'd started at L'Etoile and they loved her kind but firm approach.

'It's lovely to see you, girls. Some very familiar faces here.' She paused, looking at the actresses among the group, but I'm looking forward to getting to know all of you much better as the year goes on.'

She had everyone's attention.

'And how super it is to have two of the most

starry L'Etoile students here this morning – Molly, congratulations! And Pippa – I know you've previously been in Miss Ward's group for drama, but congratulations to you too. You've both done so very well. A round of applause, please, girls!' Miss Denham continued as the class clapped their friends. 'Perhaps we should start with the *OK!* Magazine visit. I'm sure you've got lots of questions?'

'Do Mum and Dad know about it?' Molly asked immediately. In the past, her mum had never much minded about any press attention she and Maria received, but her dad had always been a bit more reluctant.

'Of course, Molly, dear,' Miss Denham replied. 'The same goes for you, Pippa. Madame Ruby would never make an announcement like that without running it by your parents first. But this *OK!* shoot isn't going to be intrusive for any of you. They're coming to get shots of the Christmas concert, that is all. There will be more photos of the two of you in the actual article, but hopefully you won't even notice them being taken.'

'Did Dad really agree to this?' Molly asked.

'I think Dad's had to get over his phobia of sharing his daughters with the rest of the world, Moll, given your chosen career and the fact that your beautiful face is about to grace every cinema screen in the country,' Maria said proudly.

'Ahh, thanks, Mimi,' Molly said.

'I don't think I'll ever get used to the attention!' Pippa said. She'd been totally blown away when Madame Ruby had called her name that morning. She'd never thought for a moment one of the two girls the headmistress had mentioned in assembly would be her.

'Oh, Pippa, you're just amazing!' Lydia Ambrose said in awe. 'Please can we hear your track?'

'Ooooh, yes! Can we?' Daisy Mansfield asked.

Pippa looked at Miss Denham.

'I don't see why not!' Miss Denham said. 'Have you got a copy with you, Pippa? I'd love to hear what all the fuss is about!'

'Actually I haven't got it here. I . . .' Pippa began.

'Actually, Humble-but-Brilliant-Burrows . . . that's your new name, by the way,' Maria said fondly, 'the memory stick you left with Danya last night – I had to confiscate it this morning in order to get her to assembly, so I just happen to have it right here!'

'Oh, go on then!' Pippa said, resigning herself to the fact that it would be out in the open soon anyway. 'But you all have to swear you won't tell anyone you've heard it.'

'It's a deal!' Alice Parks shouted at the top of her voice.

'I think I might faint!' Belle Brown said, jumping up for a front row seat next to Maria's laptop.

'Hold on a sec – who are you?' Pippa said, suddenly panicked by an unfamiliar face in the group.

'I ... erm ... I ...' a tall, blonde girl started nervously.

'Oh, my goodness. Where are our manners?' Miss Denham said. 'I'm so sorry, my dear. I am completely guilty of getting swept up in all the excitement this morning! Girls, this is Ellie Gornall, our newest L'Etoilette.'

'Hello,' Ellie said.

'Ellie joins us from Lakewood High School and is an exquisite ballerina!' Miss Denham explained.

'Hi, Ellie!' Belle said quickly from the row behind where Ellie was sitting. 'I'm Belle. I'm majoring in ballet too! I'll show you around, if you like.'

'How kind, Belle,' Miss Denham said. 'Would you like that, Ellie?'

'That would be wonderful. Thank you so much,' Ellie said, relieved to have a friend to cling to until she knew her way around. She turned to Pippa. 'I won't breathe a word about the song, I promise.'

'OK, cool. And, sorry, Ellie. To single you out like that, I mean. My head's all over the place at the minute. This whole thing is turning me a bit crazy,' Pippa said, immediately putting Ellie at ease.

'Are we good to go then?' Maria said.

'Hit it!' Pippa said, as the class watched first the personalised message from One Direction and then her studio performance with the band.

Christmas-time for you and for me
Christmas-time for family
And if you don't know where to go
Meet me under the mistletoe

'Bravo!' Miss Denham exclaimed as the screen went black.

'I'm in love,' Danya said, the gooey look returning to her eyes.

'Danya, how do you know all the words? You only heard it for the first time last night!' Molly said.

'You have no idea!' Honey answered. 'I know all the words too – having heard them on repeat blasting from Danya's headphones all night. We literally learned them in our sleep!'

'Pippa, you're too cool for school!' Amanda Lloyd said. 'Do you need any help putting together an arrangement for this Christmas concert?'

'And will the boys come?' Belle said, voicing what they were all thinking.

'Yes, please, Amanda, to the first question, and not a chance, Belle, to the second!' Pippa said, laughing. 'Lara, do you reckon you could drum it?'

'Of course I could,' Lara said happily.

'Do you think you could write some cello or bass in so I can play too?' Lydia said.

'Definitely! I'll throw in a whole strings section. It will be so much more authentic if we can nail the whole track ourselves without any backing music,' Pippa said, already starting to hear the new arrangement in her head.

'Amazing!' Lydia said.

'OK! OK! Moving on! Let's talk ice-trekking in the south of France!' Danya said.

'Ice-trekking indeed. Whatever next?' Miss Denham said, raising an eyebrow. 'I'm sensing you girls aren't too keen on Madame Ruby's latest idea. I thought that would be right up your street, given your history of . . . shall we say . . . adventure?'

'With all due respect, Miss Denham,' Maria said, 'it's one thing going on an adventure around L'Etoile in the dark where your biggest threat is a student dressed up as a ghost, but it's quite another surviving in sub-zero temperatures halfway up a mountain with goodness knows what kind of wild animals for company!'

'I understand your trepidation, but I can reassure you that I've seen the expedition maps myself, and the terrain, albeit a little hilly in places, is relatively smooth. With all your adventuring experience, I should think you'll *walk* this expedition!' Miss Denham said with a little chuckle to herself.

'What are we going to wear?' Molly said. 'I don't think any of my leotards are going to come in particularly useful.'

'That's a good question, Molly,' Miss Denham answered.

'I reckon that's the first time in history Molly's clothing concerns have been relevant,' Maria giggled.

'Having spoken to Madame Pierre when she visited at the start of the week to brief the staff, I'm told that everything you need in terms of camping equipment – such as tents, sleeping bags, rucksacks and cooking equipment – you'll be provided with on-site when you get to France. With regards to clothing, there are lots of suitable items in your school kit,' Miss Denham said, grabbing a uniform list from her desk.

'How is that possible?' Molly said. She couldn't

remember buying any school regulation snow boots, hiking boots, snow suits, thermal underwear, fake fur hats, scarves and gloves, to name but a few of the things she might consider as *outdoorsy all-weather essentials!*

'Let's see,' Miss Denham said, reading down the page. 'Things for each student to pack. Your L'Etoile sports tracksuits – you have two of those in your kit so one for each day of the expedition. Your winter boots have perfectly suitable all-terrain soles, and your school duffle-coats are extremely warm and water-resistant . . .'

'Water-resistant!' Molly said.

'Molly's right!' Honey said. 'We'll be freezing! And if it decides to rain the whole weekend we're there, which I'm in no doubt it will, we'll be soaked to the skin!'

'Honestly, girls, I don't think it's going to be as bad as you imagine. Madame Ruby would never put any of you in danger,' Miss Denham said, not overly convincingly. 'Look, how about I report your clothing concerns back and request some waterproofs and thermals, just in case. Would that help allay your fears?'

'It's a start. Also I'm not keen to wear out my

school uniform. Do you think there would be any objection to us ordering our own hiking boots and jackets?' Molly suggested. She refused to be *outfit unprepared*!

'I can't see why not. I would imagine you'll have to sew a L'Etoile school badge onto any outer clothing so that you can be easily identified by the general public but you can collect those from Mrs Fuller's office. All right?' Miss Denham said.

'Thank you,' Molly and Honey said together.

There was no way either of them were going to be beaten by the elements, Story-seeker!

'So if there's nothing else at the moment, girls, you'd best get off to geography, where Miss Page is waiting to commence your orienteering instruction! We'll make Christopher Colombuses of you yet!' Miss Denham said, only to be met with a groan.

'Cheer up, ladies. It could be worse – you could be off to the Antarctic! Imagine the wardrobe issues you'd have then!'

5

A Lesson in Positivity!

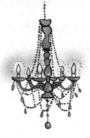

'Miss Page! How are you feeling?' Alice said, on seeing their lovely old form tutor.

'I'm on the mend, thank you, Alice,' Miss Page said. Then, addressing the rest of the class, as they filed in: 'I'm so sorry I wasn't here for you all at the end of last year. Such a terrible spot of luck!' Miss Page said.

Miss Page, if you remember, Story-seeker, had suffered a dreadful skiing accident that Easter and broken practically every bone in her body, meaning she couldn't be with her form, 3 Alpha, during the dreaded summer exam term. They'd all missed her terribly and were happy to have her back!

'But I hear that you all sailed through your exams. Well done! If I've learned anything this year, it's not what you do in the face of adversity, but how you pick yourself up and carry on after it's passed,' she said thoughtfully, as the girls took their seats.

'Now as you all know, you'll be in groups of no more than six for your expedition teams, and if I may offer one piece of advice, it would be that it's better for you to have as many team members as possible. You'll have lots of equipment to carry, and in this instance six pairs of hands will be far better than one!' Miss Page said.

'Do you want us to work out our groups now?' Belle said, putting her hand on Ellie's arm. 'Ellie's new here and I'd like her in my group if she's happy with that?'

'Oh, yes, Ellie Gornall isn't it? Welcome to L'Etoile, dear,' Miss Page said.

'Thank you, Miss Page,' Ellie said.

'I see the lovely Belle has taken you under her wing so I'd say you're in very safe hands, Ellie.'

'Yes, thank you!' Ellie said.

'Perfect. Who else would like to join Belle and Ellie?' she said. She looked around the room, only to discover that the class had already sat itself quite naturally into two groups of six.

On one side, there were the BFFs (as she'd so often heard the girls refer to themselves), consisting of Maria, Molly, Honey, Danya, Pippa and Sally. And on the other, Belle, Ellie, Amanda, Alice, Lydia and Lara.

'I see. OK, so we seem to already have two quite formidable groups of six. Is that right?'

The girls nodded. There was a good mix of skills on both teams.

'Excellent. Very evenly balanced I'd say,' Miss Page said, knowing her students as well as she did. Now let me ask you, has anyone any previous orienteering experience?' she asked.

'Before I started at L'Etoile, I spent most of my summers camping around England with Mum and Uncle Harry, if that counts?' Pippa volunteered.

'So you'd be able to pitch a tent then?' Miss Page said.

'With my eyes shut in a thunderstorm!' Pippa said confidently, remembering a soggy holiday spent in the Lake District a few years ago.

'Great!' Danya said. 'A crucial skill tick in the box for Team BFF!'

'Team BFF! Love it!' Pippa said.

'I've done my fair share of camping too so that should be good for Team Belle,' Amanda said quickly, keen to put a tick in the box for her team.

'Fantastic, Mands!' Belle said, not quite sure how her group had suddenly become Team Belle.

'Anyone else?' Miss Page said, keen to gauge how much the girls had to learn.

'I've become quite handy with a compass from our sailing holidays,' Danya said. 'Dad always leaves me in charge of that to keep us right when we're on the yacht.'

'Good,' Miss Page said. 'That will be a crucial skill to keep you on the right path. Sometimes every direction looks the same when you're surrounded by water – or indeed trees and mountains in this case.'

'It just gets more and more appealing by the minute,' Molly groaned under her breath.

'I've flown all the way to Singapore without the in-flight entertainment working. Does that count as roughing it?' Sally said.

The whole class burst out laughing.

'And I can navigate my way out of most detentions so that's got to be a plus!' Maria giggled.

'Yes, yes. Very good, girls. I'm happy to see you haven't all completely lost your sense of humour over this. Look, I know it's the unknown, and the unknown is daunting, but let's not forget what Madame Ruby said. This is a team-building exercise, for you to bond through *survival*,' Miss Page said.

'Survival? I'll say it's survival . . . wearing the same pair of shoes for two days in a row!' Honey said.

'And finding a hairdo to survive two days in all weathers with no electricity for my hairdryer!' Molly agreed.

The class giggled again – but only half-heartedly this time.

Let's face it, Story-seeker, L'Étoile students are far more at home backstage than on a campsite.

'I've done it before, actually,' came a small voice. It was the new girl, Ellie.

'Camping?' Miss Page said. 'That's marvellous, Ellie. You must . . .'

But Ellie interrupted her.

'No, sorry, not just camping. Chateau Pierre. I did it a couple of years ago at my last school,' she explained.

'You did?' Belle said. 'Wicked! Now I'm even more excited you're on our team!'

'Wow – how cool is that? We're sure to have the upper hand now!' Lara said excitedly.

'Just brilliant!' Maria said to Danya, and none too quietly. 'If we ever had any advantage at all, given our combined super-brain status, Team BFF has just been kicked off the leaderboard by Belle's Beagles!'

'Belle's Beagles!' Belle squealed with delight. 'Love that!'

'I know, how is that even fair?' Danya whispered back.

'Bet she forgot to mention that little fact at her interview with old Ruby!' Pippa said.

'Actually, I did mention it,' Ellie said, overhearing. 'As soon as Madame Ruby told me and my parents what she had in store for L'Etoile this term, I told her I'd already been on one of the expeditions, but she said it would be highly unlikely I'd end up doing the same route and not to worry.'

'Right. Fine.' Pippa blushed, feeling guilty for being mean to the new girl. She had been that new girl once upon a time.

'Well, I think it's wonderful,' Miss Page said. 'And don't forget, girls. Just because you're on different teams within your year groups, you're all still on Team L'Etoile and it would serve you all to help each other should the need arise. Now if there are no more questions, I'll give you the new lesson schedules. It won't come as any surprise that the first few weeks will focus on orienteering with me and various other outdoor pursuits with Mr Hart, to get you all ready for France. You'll need to be prepared for all situations in all weathers.'

There was that word again. Weather. Molly wanted the facts. 'Excuse me, but what will the weather be like when we go?'

'It's difficult to say for sure, Molly, but temperatures do appear to be dropping quite rapidly. That said, there hasn't been too much rain at Chateau Pierre of late . . .'

'How long have we got before our year go?' Lydia asked.

'Of course! Silly me. I quite forgot. You're not going for a few weeks yet,' Miss Page said. 'The younger years need to go ahead of you, before it gets too—' And she stopped herself.

'Too cold?' Molly said quickly. 'I knew it! We're going to get frostbite out there!'

If ever there was a moment Molly Fitzfoster lost her sparkle, this just might be it, Story-seeker.

'Don't be daft, Moll,' Maria said. 'We'll be absolutely fine – and you know why? Because with our research expertise and your gold medal in online shopping, we're going to be kitted out to perfection!'

Molly managed a small smile in her sister's direction.

'Now if that's everything, we'll start with a little map reading. Would you all grab a map from the clear box on my desk and I'll come to see you a group at a time?' Miss Page said.

'Anyone else got a really bad feeling about this?' Danya whispered to the girls.

'Yep!' Pippa said. 'But then I usually do!'

'So the aim of the game in these few weeks before you leave for Parc du Mercantour,' Miss Page said in her very best French, 'is for me to give you the start and end points and for you to map out your route. You can do as much research about the area as you wish, to make your job as easy as possible when you're on the ground . . .'

'Like finding out where the nearest accident and emergency unit is?' Sally said with a groan.

Sally is well known for being clumsy, Story-seeker, and she didn't much fancy her chances hiking in snow and ice!

'Come on, girls. Buck up! This is going to be fun!' Miss Page insisted. She'd have those girls ready in time for their trip, if it was the last thing she did!

6

An Unfair Advantage

As the days and weeks flew by in a flurry of guy ropes and French dictionaries, the majority of L'Etoile students were looking forward to their stint *dans les Alpes.*

The two French teachers, Mademoiselle Cochon (Miss Piggy in English, which never ceased to amuse the girls, partly due to an unfortunately turned-up nose) and Madame Flaubert, had worked their socks off with the students to polish up their grasp of the French language before their departure.

'To finish your crash course in French, what number would you dial from a phone box, should you need the emergency services?'

Maria looked blankly at Danya and the others, but no one seemed to know.

'Wait for it . . . three – two – one . . . there she goes!' Sally whispered, seeing Ellie's hand shoot up for the fifth time that lesson.

'*Oui*, Ellie?' Mademoiselle Cochon asked.

'Is it 112?' Ellie said. 'I think it's the same emergency number across Europe actually.'

'*Oui*, Ellie. *Excellent, ma petite*,' Mademoiselle Cochon praised. 'That is correct.'

'So, girls, Madame Cochon and I would like to wish you *bon chance*. Try to use your French as much as possible. There is no substitute for learning a language by using it in the country itself! You are dismissed!' Madame Flaubert said.

'What is it about that girl? It's like there's nothing she doesn't know about France or roughing it!' Danya said as the girls walked back to Garland at the end of a long week's training.

'It's just because she's been there and done it before. Imagine what knowledge you'd be able to bring to the team if you were her,' Honey said. 'You only need to go somewhere once to remember how to get back there.'

'True,' Danya said. 'But what's annoying is that I actually like the girl! It would be so much easier if I couldn't stand her.'

'Girls!!' Heavenly Smith from 4 Beta said, appearing behind them. 'Have you heard the gossip – about Ellie?'

'No!' Maria and Danya exploded together.

'What is it?' Pippa said.

'Nancy just got an email from her mum who's spent all afternoon at a charity event and guess who the guest speaker was?' Heavenly said.

'Erm . . . might need a bit of a clue here,' Maria said. 'It could be anyone!'

'OK, OK – Wolf Gornall!' Heavenly said.

'Wolf Gornall? The adventurer and survival expert?' Maria said.

Molly, Honey, Sally and Pippa looked at Maria. They'd never heard of this Wolf man in their lives.

'Yes!' Heavenly said, gazing at their blank faces.

'And this is gossip, why?' Danya said. She had also heard of the explorer but couldn't understand why he might have got the L'Etoile gossip mill turning.

'Did you say his surname's Gornall?' Honey said suddenly.

'Yes . . . you're getting warmer . . . keep going,' Heavenly said.

'As in Ellie Gornall!' Betsy Harris said, popping up behind Heavenly.

'No way! No wonder the girl's an outdoor genius. It's in her blood!' Maria said. 'Talk about an unfair advantage!'

'I'm not sure whether that's made me feel better or worse!' Danya said. 'Better that she's genetically built to be better at this stuff than me, or worse because we haven't a hope of beating her and Belle's Beagles to the finish line.'

'Goodness me, this is really getting to you, isn't it?' Honey said, giving her sister a squeeze. 'You don't need to be first at every single thing you do, Dan. Honestly, you don't. Maybe if you can get your head around that, you might enjoy life a bit more.'

'Wow. OK. Thanks for that, sis. I'll remember that next time you want help getting top marks again,' Danya said, a little hurt.

'Girls, girls. Look. Knowing this about Ellie doesn't change anything,' Maria said. 'We've absolutely nailed our route and I feel confident in saying there's nothing I don't know about Parc du Mercantour! I must have looked through a thousand photos of the area. Once

Albie arrives with our new outdoors wardrobe, we'll be all set!'

'What time is Albie getting here, Moll?' Sally asked.

Albie Good, Story-seeker, if you remember, is the www.looklikeastar.com delivery boy who's been delivering to the Fitzfoster girls since they placed their first clothing order many moons ago. He's become a good friend to the girls and they can always rely on him to help them out when they need it!

'Six o'clock tonight,' Molly said. 'Because of the extra bits and pieces we asked him to pick up for us from London, he needed to wait until he could borrow the company van to put it all in. He wouldn't have got enough kit for one of us on the back of his bike, much less for all of us!'

'I hope we've ordered enough stuff,' Molly said, unlocking their bedroom door.

'There aren't enough products on the market for you two to consider you have enough things to wear!' Sally said, with a grin.

'Ha! Ha! Very funny . . .' Molly stopped dead as she entered the room.

'MUM!' she exclaimed.

'What?' Maria pushed her way through. 'Mum! What on earth are you doing here?'

Molly and Maria collapsed into Linda Fitzfoster's arms. Never had they been so pleased to see her.

'Oh, darlings. It's so lovely to see your little faces. Dad and I do miss you so much during term-time. Albie phoned the house this afternoon in a panic. The van broke down this morning in Watford and they didn't expect it to be back on the road again until at least Monday so I jumped at the excuse to pop down and see you under the guise of being your Friday delivery boy!' Mrs Fitzfoster said, giving Sally, Pippa and the Sawyer twins a hug too.

'Mum, that's so cool of you,' Molly said, looking around the room. 'But I don't understand. Where is all the stuff?'

'Have you any idea just how much you ordered, Molly Fitzfoster?' Linda asked as she raised one eyebrow.

Molly winced. She had no idea how she managed to get away with spending what she did on fashion, but most of the time her parents weren't there to see it all arrive. This might be a different story!

'Luckily, the Bentley has a boot the size of a small transit van, and we were able to get it all in, but we had to unpack it first. Miss Coates has let me use the second-year common room as a dressing room for you, since they're in France doing their expedition today. You want to see it?'

'Yes!' The girls squealed and ran down the Garland corridor to the common room block.

'Tah-dah!' Linda Fitzfoster said, as she switched on the light.

'No way!' Molly said.

'Coooool!' Pippa said.

'Perfect!' Maria muttered.

The girls' eyes travelled over the six stylish, warm hiking outfits laid out for them, from waterproof hats to the funkiest hiking boots. At their feet were matching sleeping bags, complete with their initials and TEAM BFF written underneath.

'But . . . when did you have time to do all this?' Maria said.

'And how did you know what we've called our team?!' Danya said, bewildered.

'Molly, you mentioned it when we Skyped on Monday night. It stuck in my mind as I had no idea what BFF meant and had to go and look it up. The letters are only ironed on, mind, not embroidered, as I'd have liked, but Maggie and I didn't have much time this afternoon, so this will just have to do! Do you like it?' Linda said.

'It's sooooo great. Thanks, Mum! You're the best,' Molly said.

'How is my mum?' Sally asked, hearing her mother's name and wishing she could have been here too. 'Is she OK?'

'I'm fine, darling,' came a voice from behind.

'Mum!' Sally cried, swinging around and launching herself at her mum for a cuddle. 'You're here!'

'Of course. I couldn't let Mrs F manage all this lot by herself, could I? It might say 'lightweight' on all the gear but put it all together and it's jolly heavy,' Maggie Sudbury said as she stroked her daughter's hair.

Sally's mum, Maggie, if you remember Story-seeker, has worked for the Fitzfosters for the past couple of years, since she was sacked by the Marciano family. And as part of Maggie's salary, Sally got to stay on at L'Etoile with the girls. Everyone was a winner!

'Well, you've done a great job, Mum!'

'Yes, thank you!' Honey, Danya and Pippa said together, secretly longing for hugs from their own mothers.

'The only thing you'll need to do yourselves is to collect some L'Etoile school logo patches from Mrs Fuller. All the parents got an email giving permission to send in extra supplies for their girls, just so long as you can still be easily recognised as L'Etoile students.'

'Let's try it on!' Molly said, racing over to the outfit that had the letters M.F. on the right breast pocket.

'Moll, I don't think we've got time. We're already going to be late for supper and you know how Miss Coates gets. I can't face a whole weekend in her bad books!' Maria said.

'Actually, Maria, I've cleared it with Miss Coates for you all to have supper with Maggie and I this evening in the little Garland kitchen. Maggie's made toad-in-the-hole!' Linda Fitzfoster said with a huge grin.

'You're kidding! This just gets better!' Molly squealed.

'Almost makes the ice expedition worth it!' Honey grinned.

'I knew I could smell something amazing!!' Sally said, sniffing the air.

'Toad-in-the-hole! Yum!' Pippa said, her mouth watering.

'It'll make a change from the usual Friday supper of a bread roll in the Ivy Room, followed by a cola bottle and crisp midnight feast!' Danya said, forgetting she was in the company of parents.

'Danya!' Maria said.

'Only joking!' Danya said quickly. 'I meant with . . . errrm, *milk* bottles – you know, a healthy calcium-filled bottle of milk and crispy . . . errr, crispy kale vegetable accompaniment to whatever delicious protein fuelled meal Mrs Mackle has cooked for us!'

The whole room, including Linda and Maggie, fell apart laughing.

'Too much?' Danya said with a giggle.

'Way too much, sis!' Honey said.

And with that, the girls set about trying on all their new gear, while Maggie prepared a Friday night feast to rival all others.

♡

'Your mums are so cool,' Danya and Honey said, as the girls sat chatting in their pyjamas that night.

'Aren't they?' Molly said. 'I wish you'd been able to see yours too.'

'Me too. Thank goodness for Skype. Always makes them seem so much closer when you can't get the real thing,' Pippa said.

'Definitely,' Danya said.

'So this is it then, our last weekend before France! Goodness only knows what icy crevice I'll have fallen down by this time next week!' Sally said.

'Sal!!' Pippa said. 'Remember what Wolf Gornall says. PMA!'

'I know! Positive mental attitude! Got it!' Sally answered, rolling her eyes.

'Night, Team BFF!' Pippa said.

'Night!'

7

France, Here We Come!

'Can you believe we're driving all the way to France?!' Molly moaned as they made their way to the back of the coach where Pippa had saved the last few rows.

'What on earth are you talking about?' Honey said. 'Miss Page must have talked about the travel plan at least a dozen times over the past few weeks. The coach is taking us as far as the airport and then we're flying into Nice.'

'Oh, thank goodness for that! I was wondering how we were going to complete such a trip in one day,' Molly said. She was feeling particularly ditsy that morning.

'Molly, you really need to listen. I don't know how you manage to just switch off like that!' Honey said.

'I don't know either,' Molly answered. 'But that's exactly what it's like. Whenever I'm being given crucial instructions about anything other than dancing, acting or singing, it's as if a switch automatically goes off in my head. I can't seem to control it.'

'Well, you'd better find a way of engaging that switch for the next few days or you're going to end up lost on a mountain!' Honey grinned.

'You wouldn't leave me . . . would you?' Molly asked in a panic.

'Of course I wouldn't!' Honey said, squeezing her BFF's arm. 'But let's all try and stay switched on – at least until we get home. You wouldn't want to miss your own première!'

If that didn't get Molly's attention, Story-seeker, nothing would!

'Right then. I think that's everyone. Miss Ward, would you let the driver know we're ready to leave?' Miss

Denham called out to the 4 Beta form tutor, having checked the entire fourth year off her list.

'Of course, Miss Denham. Just one second . . .' Miss Ward said, as she tapped the last girl to pass her on the shoulder.

'Lydia, tell me you haven't brought your cello with you. There's just not enough room for it, dear. I'm very sorry, but it's going to have to stay here,' Miss Ward said as Lydia reluctantly handed over her beloved cello, Velvet.

'Mrs Fu-ller!' Miss Ward called to the deputy headmistress, while waving Velvet in the air. 'Would you be kind enough to ask Miss Coates to put this safely back in Lydia Ambrose's room. Honestly, whatever next?'

Mrs Fuller nodded as she turned and waved at Miss Coates to explain.

'But I've never been apart from Velvet!' Lydia moaned as she sat next to Lara, who was more than a little relieved not to be sharing her seat with Lydia and her enormous cello.

'Don't you worry, Lydia,' Lara said. 'Just think how free you'll feel. That's why I took up the drums. No chance of carting those around everywhere you go. Cheer up. We're off to France!!'

And before the girls had chance to notice, the coach was cruising along the motorway and their journey to Parc du Mercantour had begun.

The fourth-year girls remained seated in their expedition teams for the remainder of the day, not even splitting up as they huddled together on the aeroplane waiting to take off.

'Erm . . . this might be a good time to mention that I'm absolutely terrified of flying!' Pippa announced, squeezing Sally's hand until her fingers turned white.

'Oh, Pippa, don't be daft. Flying is the safest way to travel these days. Honestly,' Sally said, imploring the others with her eyes to find a way of distracting their friend.

'Yes . . . that's right,' Honey said, thinking on her feet. 'In fact, now might also be a good time to tell you we'd like you to be our Team Leader!'

'Team what?' Maria and Danya exclaimed together.

'Team LEAD-ER!' Molly said, cottoning on to what Honey was trying to do. 'Wouldn't Pippa be perfect, Mimi?'

Maria was mortified. She'd never been on a project she hadn't controlled from start to finish. She didn't know what to say.

'Oh . . . errrr . . . right. Yes, we were saying that, weren't we? Pippa for Team Leader,' Danya said begrudgingly.

'Maria?' Molly said.

'Yes. Pippa for Team Leader. Makes perfect sense,' Maria said, with just a hint of sarcasm.

'Yes, Pips. We thought you'd be best to head up Team BFF, given all your previous camping experience,' Molly said.

'What do you say?' Honey asked her.

To Sally's relief, Pippa loosened her grip on her hand as she smiled and said she'd be honoured.

'Actually, I've been thinking that we need an expedition song!' Pippa said.

'An expedition song?' Molly asked excitedly. 'What sort of expedition song?'

'You know the sort of thing. Like a military-style one that army cadets sing when they're on outdoor manoeuvres,' Pippa explained.

'That sounds like fun!' Belle piped up from the row behind.

'Butt out, Belle, with all due respect!' Danya cried.

'Make up your own chant!'

'Danya!' Honey exclaimed. 'No need to be so rude!'

'What?!' Danya said. She couldn't help being competitive. It was in her blood. She turned to the others. 'Can't we at least have one up on Belle's Beagles and Wolfette with the great Pippa Burrows on our team?'

'I'm guessing I'm Wolfette?' Ellie said, her head popping from the row in front of them.

'Ooops,' Honey said under her breath.

'Sorry, Ellie. I think it's a cool name,' Danya said. She'd forgotten the new girl was sitting within hearing distance.

'Actually, I love it! And as far as song-writing goes, my mum happens to be Madonna!' Ellie said.

'You're kidding!' Danya exploded.

'Yes, I'm kidding.' Ellie *Wolfette* Gornall giggled. 'Don't worry, Danya, the Gornall family is *not* known for our musical ability!'

'YES!' Danya said with a twinkle in her eyes. 'Hit it, Pippa!'

Pippa began to chant, tapping out the beat on the back of the seat in front.

Team BFF, we're on our way
Hiking is our favourite play
Preparation is a must
We're Team BFF, so eat our dust!

The whole plane had gone quiet to listen to Pippa and a round of applause sounded.

'Ha! Pippa! Brilliant!' Danya said. 'Beat that, Belle's Beagles!'

'We just might,' Belle said and set about with the rest of her team to work on their own song.

'Give us strength, Elise,' Miss Denham whispered to Miss Ward, despairing at the competitive atmosphere swirling around their girls.

'I don't know if it's strength we need or just earplugs. Their eyes are on the prize, that's for sure,' Miss Ward whispered back.

♡

Thankfully, Nice airport was fairly quiet, which had enabled the two teachers to deliver the girls and their luggage to the coach without too much drama. The only remaining challenge for Miss Ward and Miss Denham when they arrived at Chateau Pierre an hour later was the incessant, rowdy chanting as each team tried to out-sing the others.

'May we have some quiet please, girls?' Miss Denham said, attempting to talk above the noise as the coach drew to a halt outside the chateau walls.

'Please, girls, listen to Miss—' Miss Ward started, only to be interrupted by the shrillest whistle she'd ever heard.

'Thank you, *Monsieur le Conducteur*!' Miss Denham said gratefully to the driver, as silence at last fell upon the bus. 'Before we arrive at Chateau Pierre, I want to remind you that as long as you are away from L'Etoile, you are ambassadors for the school and should demonstrate exceptional behaviour at all times. Is that understood?' she warned sternly.

The whole coach nodded, ready to represent their beloved school as well as they possibly could.

'Right then! *On y va!*' she announced, which meant something like 'Let's go!' in French. She just hoped she'd pronounced it correctly!

8

Chateau Pierre

As the coach rattled down the long driveway to Chateau Pierre, every L'Etoile girl had their nose pressed against a window, trying to make out their surroundings in the misty darkness. Night had already fallen, but once they entered the floodlit car park they saw four other coaches already parked up with name-plates in the back windows.

'St George's College,' Molly read.

'Forest Hill School,' Pippa said.

'Claremont College,' Honey said.

'And Lakewood High School,' Maria said, as she watched a large group of girls waiting for their luggage to be off-loaded.

'Ellie!' Belle cried suddenly. 'Lakewood High. Isn't that your old school?'

'Yes, it is!' she said. 'What a coincidence!'

'WATC!' Molly said to Maria.

WATC = What are the chances? Story-seeker.

'I can't believe it!' Ellie said, craning her neck for a better view. 'I wonder if it's my old year group?'

'That would be really useful. At least you'll be able to give us the inside track on their strengths and weaknesses!' Danya said.

'Danya!' Honey said, knowing exactly the way her twin's mind worked.

'What?!' Danya said. 'It would be good to know what we're up against.'

'Yeah, like we'd share that with Team BFF!' Belle said.

'OK, girls. *Nous sommes arrivées!*' Miss Ward said, in a slightly better French accent than Miss Denham. 'Watch your step as you leave the coach. Our driver has said it's a little bit icy underfoot, so pay attention and no running.'

'FGS. If we can't cross a car park without falling over, how are we going to manage hiking up a mountain?' Molly groaned.

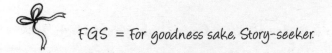

'Can someone hold onto my arm?' Sally asked. 'I don't want to break any bones before I've even entered the chateau!'

Pippa grabbed Sally. 'Here we go then, girls. Team BFF . . . group hands!' Pippa said as the six girls piled their right hands one on top of the other and raised them in the air.

'Whoop!' they shouted, and collected their things together to go.

♡

'Lara's Lurchers would have been a much stronger name than Belle's Beagles,' Lara whispered to Amanda as the L'Etoilettes stood in the car park, waiting to be reunited with their luggage.

'Oooh, that would have been a good one,' Amanda said. 'My uncle breeds lurchers. They're adaptable to all kinds of terrains and known for their stealth and intelligence!'

'Exactly like us!' Lara giggled.

'Oh my days, it's freeeezing out here!' Betsy said with a shiver. 'I'm now wishing I'd taken my mum up on her offer to post my ski jacket down.'

'Don't worry, Betsy,' Fashion Faye from 4 Beta said. 'I've brought a couple of spares with me that my sisters have grown out of. One of those should fit you.'

'Oh, thanks, Faye! You're a lifesaver,' Betsy said.

'That's what I like to see, L'Etoile girls sticking together!' Ellie said, hearing Faye's kind words. 'Can't see the point in us being in direct competition, what with all these other schools we're up against!'

'Agreed,' Betsy said. 'What's your team called by the way, Faye?'

'Team Mars!' Faye said sheepishly. She'd thought it sounded a bit daft, but Daisy had insisted she'd read somewhere that an adventurer survived a whole month lost in the wild with only Mars Bars and rainwater to keep them alive.

'How about your team, Betsy?' Daisy asked, overhearing the conversation and hoping it wasn't cooler than Team Mars.

'Team Swift!' Betsy said.

'Oooh, that's a good one, guys,' Daisy said, enviously. 'Does exactly what it says on the tin, doesn't it.'

'Which way now?' Maria said, having loaded herself up with all her stuff.

'Miss Ward is waiting around the other side of the coach for you with a Madame Renard, if you're ready. Madame Renard is our main point of contact at Chateau Pierre, so remember her face.

'Madame Renard . . . Mrs Fox . . . what is it with the French and animal surnames?' Lottie said, with a giggle.

'Yes, thank you, Lottie,' Miss Denham said abruptly. 'You can make your way round to them now, but don't go charging ahead. We need to wait for Lakewood High School to check in first. I can't lose any of you before you've even crossed the start line!'

'Cool. Ready, Team BFF?' Maria said.

'Shouldn't that be my line, as leader?' Pippa said. She wondered whether this was how Mr Potts might feel in January when he took over L'Etoile from Madame Ruby. Even though they'd both been given the top job, both knew full well there would be plenty of others behind the scenes, pulling their strings!

'Of course. Forgive me, Pips. Just habit!' Maria said graciously.

Pippa nodded. She was going to have to rule this lot with an iron fist.

'Follow me then, gang,' Pippa said, trying not to let her chattering teeth lessen her authority. Leaders must be strong!

It truly was icy-cold. Sally, despite holding onto Pippa, predictably managed to lose her balance in the first ten steps she'd taken in France. That didn't bode well for the mountain! But after almost ten hours spent on various modes of transport, everyone was relieved to be out in the fresh air – even if it was cold enough to burn the inside of their nostrils.

'L'Etoile, your accommodation is on the ground floor of the west wing,' announced Madame Renard, a tall brunette woman with a pinched face and weather-beaten cheeks. 'Once Lakewood have cleared the car park you can go ahead. Go to front entrance and turn left.'

Unfortunately only Belle's Beagles were close enough to hear the instructions. Those who were still walking around the coach at the time had been stopped in their tracks by a fracas happening alongside the Lakewood High coach.

'That's mine!' shrieked a tall, strong-looking girl with an American accent.

'No, if . . .' came a muffled response, which they couldn't really make out.

The American girl shouted again. 'Kate! Get over here and tell Miss Hollywood to get her thieving paws off my stuff.'

A small, wiry girl with straggly red hair, answering

to the name of Kate, scurried into the middle of the Lakewood High circle of girls.

The L'Etoile girls crouched down, peering through the group of Lakewood legs in an attempt to see what was going on. On the ground, another girl in a dark-hooded puffa jacket sat, scrambling together the contents of a spilled rucksack.

'That's a bit unkind,' Danya whispered.

'How horrible,' Pippa whispered back. 'Where are their teachers?'

'I can't see any,' Maria said.

'That poor girl!' Sally said, joining the others.

The onlookers stood up straight again, trying to see where Kate had gone.

'There she is!' Honey said, pointing to the redhead on the left of the tall, American girl.

Kate didn't look as mouse-like as before. She seemed to stand taller, shaking her head and grinning in the direction of the girl, freezing on the ground.

'It's not? Oh yeah. That rucksack's black. Mine's red. 'Course it's not my stuff. My bad!' the American girl said, flicking her hair behind her shoulders and marching towards the Chateau entrance. The rest of the Lakewood girls followed. Everyone, that is, except the girl on the floor.

'Can you believe that just happened?' Autumn said to Maria. 'It's just horrible!'

'Do you think we should go and help her?' Maria said to Danya, but before they had a chance to move, Madame Renard was already at the girl's side and helping her to her feet.

'That's that then,' Danya said. 'We're going to have to watch Lakewood High! Where's Ellie and her Lakewood knowledge when you need her?'

'Belle's Beagles have already gone in. I don't think they saw any of that,' Pippa said. 'I think we should go too. There's nothing we can do to help now.'

The remaining L'Etoile girls headed for the entrance, leaving Madame Renard to help the girl repack her rucksack. Only Sally lingered. There had been something about the girl on the ground, but she couldn't put her finger on what it was.

'Hey!' Pippa called to her from the grand chateau entrance. 'You coming, or what?'

Hearing her voice, the girl on the ground glanced in Pippa's direction, enabling Sally to catch glimpse of her profile. She turned white as a sheet. It couldn't be. It just couldn't be! Could it?

♡ ♥ ♡

9

WATC

'Where are Pips and Sally?' Maria asked, as she searched through her rucksack for her phone charger.

'Not sure,' Danya answered. 'I don't think Sally realised we'd come in.'

'Isn't it nice we're all going to be in the same room for once? No sneaking about through "locked" doors tonight!' Honey said.

'Ah . . . there you are. Where have you b—?' Maria said. She stopped when she saw Sally's face.

'Oh no . . . Sally, did you fall over again? Tell me you haven't broken anything! We need all hands on deck if we're going to win this thing.' Danya looked her friend up and down for any obvious signs of damage.

Sally stood in silence.

'I've no idea what happened. She hasn't said a word. Let her sit so she can catch her breath,' Pippa said sharply.

'Oh, my goodness, is it something serious, Sal?' Maria asked. 'Talk to us.'

Sally was shivering. 'I . . . I can't be sure. It doesn't make any sense . . .'

'What is it?' Pippa coaxed, stroking Sally's back.

'I . . . I think the girl on the ground . . . was . . .' Sally started to cry.

Molly gasped, taking in the familiar look of terror on Sally's face. A look she hadn't seen since last year.

'You think it was Lucifette, don't you, Sal?' Molly said gravely.

Sally looked up. 'Yes, but how did you . . . ?'

'Oh, Sally. There's only one person in this world who makes you shake with fear and anger, and that's Lucinda Marciano.'

The others were silent.

'Did you speak to her?' Maria asked. 'Did she see you?'

'No . . . no . . .' Sally blubbed. 'Nothing like that. She didn't see me. In fact I can't even be sure it *was* her. She had that big hood and everything – it's just that when Pippa called me to come in, she looked up and I saw the side of her face in the light. Oh, no, I'm sure it was her. I'm telling you it was her!'

'You poor thing,' Maria said, taking control. 'You've had an awful shock. Pippa, would you take Sally to wash her face? The bathrooms are just down the corridor to the right. Don't worry about bumping into Lakewood. We saw them heading to the east wing as we came in.'

'Absolutely,' Pippa said, leading Sally away.

'Lucifette? Really?' Molly said, when they'd left the room. 'You're telling me that girl we just witnessed being bullied was the great Lucinda Marciano?'

'I don't know. Do you think Sally could just be tired and paranoid? It's been a long day for all of us,' Honey said. 'I know I can hardly think straight.'

'What is it with this Marciano girl? I've never met her, yet she seems to be a constant presence in our lives,' Danya said.

'I don't know what to say,' Maria said.

'What about asking Ellie?' Honey said.

'Now who's a fan of exploiting friends?' Danya joked.

'Honey, that's a great idea. If Lucifette is now a

student at Lakewood, she might even know her from last term, if they were both there at the same time, that is,' Maria exclaimed. 'Good work, Honey!'

Honey blushed. It wasn't often she got praise like that from brainbox Maria Fitzfoster.

'Actually, I'm sure she won't mind. I heard her saying to Betsy and Faye that us L'Etoile girls should stick together against the other schools. I bet she'll be happy to tell us everything she knows,' Molly said.

'We could ask her at supper – I heard Miss Denham telling Team Swift to be ready in twenty minutes in the corridor. They'll probably knock for us all any moment,' Pippa said.

'Even better,' Danya grinned.

♡

The canteen at Chateau Pierre was like a scene out of the *Harry Potter* movies. There were never-ending long wooden bench tables packed with students scoffing what might be their last hot meal of the weekend.

'I never thought chicken stew could taste so good!' Molly said.

'*Coq au vin!*' snapped Madame Renard, who happened to be passing with her own supper tray.

Molly smiled apologetically.

'Have you spotted her yet?' Sally said as she raced over with her tray to sit between Danya and Honey. Her usual colour had returned to her cheeks.

'Well, this is an honour!' Danya said. Sally always sat with Pippa.

'Sorry, guys. I figured if Lucifette doesn't know you two, she's unlikely to spot me sitting between you!' Sally said.

'Very clever,' Pippa noted. 'I won't be offended then.'

'I can't see where Lakewood High are sitting, can you? Even with the lights in the car park, with everyone wrapped up in their warm weather gear, I wouldn't recognise any of their faces. Everyone in here looks completely different. Now's your chance to call on Wolfette to help.' Maria nodded to where Ellie had just sat down with her own steaming tray of *coq au vin* and rice.

'Can I at least finish m—' Danya started.

'NO!' the others exclaimed and bowed their heads quickly in case they'd attracted too much attention.

'Wow! OK, OK!' Danya said and, elegant as a gazelle, she stood and swooped into the empty space next to Ellie.

'Danya?' Ellie said in surprise.

'Danya, if you're here to be rude, you can go away now,' Belle said, sticking up for her new best friend.

'I'm not, I promise. In fact, I wanted to apologise,' Danya said.

Belle raised a suspicious eyebrow.

'It's just, I get so competitive, my emotions run away with me sometimes. I'm sorry if I've offended you, Ellie,' Danya continued. 'I hear you think we should all be on some kind of uber-L'Etoile team against the other schools and I happen to think that's a good call.'

Ellie took a moment to analyse the situation and then smiled. 'Oh, that's all right. I totally get it. And please, do call me Wolfette . . . I kind of like it!'

Danya grinned back. She couldn't help but warm to this ballerina expeditioner!

'Besides, I know how you feel. I'm as competitive as they come and every bone in my body wants to win, but I've done this course before – or something like it and it's not easy. Any L'Etoile win is a win for all of us, so I'm all for sharing intel,' Ellie said with a grin.

'Sounds good,' Danya said. 'In the interests of "sharing intel", as you put it, can I pick your brains about Lakewood High?'

'Sure. What do you want to know?' Ellie said, through a mouthful of chicken.

'The lot that are here this weekend – were you in their year?' Danya asked.

Ellie put down her fork. 'To be honest, I haven't seen anyone I know yet, but then I've only really seen their coach.'

'Would you mind having a look round the canteen and seeing if you recognise anyone?' Danya asked. 'It's kind of important.'

Ellie was confused, but happy to oblige her new friends, so started scanning the room. Suddenly her gaze fell upon a familiar face at the far end of the same bench they were on.

'Oh, my goodness. Yes, it's my lot. They're all here!' She started to stand up to get their attention.

'Hold on just a sec. When you say they're *all* here – are there any Americans among them?' Danya asked.

'Um – yes, there is one, but you don't want to mess with her. Philly Malby. She's the really tall girl – sitting at the head of the table. You see her?' Ellie said, peering around behind the row of diners stretching away from her.

'Yes . . . yes, I do,' Danya said, clocking the tall girl who had been calling the shots earlier in the car park.

'Thanks, Wolfette, you've been more than helpful.'

'Any time!' Ellie said, taking one last forkful of rice and making her way towards her old school friends.

'It is the Lakewood fourth-year. Wolfette even knew the tall American girl who was doing all the shouting earlier.' Danya whispered when she got back to the others.

'Did you ask her if she knew Lucinda – if it was Lucinda?' Sally said. It all felt like a bad hallucination a few hours on.

'She said there was just one American – Philly. So I'm guessing not,' Danya said.

'But you didn't ask her outright?' Honey said in surprise.

'To be honest, by the time she'd given me the girl's name and the fact that she was the only American, that was as much as I could get out of her before she ran over to say hi to them all,' Danya said, a little sheepishly.

'So much for sharing intel! What I wouldn't give to have my laptop with me!' Maria said.

'How about using your mobile?' Molly suggested.

'Have you even checked your phone since you

arrived on this mountain? No service whatsoever!'
Maria said, exasperated.

'This is torture!' Sally groaned.

'Look, Sally. Think about it this way. If you're right, and that was Lucinda you saw, she wasn't in any shape to terrorise you, was she?' Molly said.

'Molly's right,' Pippa said. 'And I hate to say it, but if it is her, I can't help feeling a bit sorry for her. You saw what a mess she was in.'

'It's called karma!' Sally snapped. 'Karma for the bully that she was to me, to you, to everyone she's ever met!' And with that Sally darted out of the dining room.

'Come on, girls, let's go after her. We need to get a good night's sleep before this nightmare begins tomorrow anyway,' Maria said.

And the girls went back to their room to calm Sally and mentally prepare for what might be one of the toughest weekends of their lives.

10

La Grande Expedition: Day One

'*I*'ve got eye-bags big enough for a week's food shop!' Honey groaned as they stood in line to collect Team BFF's cooking equipment.

La Grande Expedition: Day One had meant an early start for everyone.

Miss Denham and Miss Ward had woken them all at six a.m. to give them enough time for a hot shower and breakfast before they had to leave. They'd then taken a couple of teams each to check that the girls had everything they needed, before leaving for base camp to collect the rest of their camping equipment.

'It's a good job there are six of us. Not sure how Team Mars is going to cope with only four of them. Look at poor Faye. She's carrying the same amount of things as we're sharing between us!' Pippa said to Sally. She could see Faye swaying under the weight of her bags.

'Hi, everyone!' Ellie called as she bounced over to the girls, dragging a sack of some sort. 'Don't you just love an early start? Best part of the day, my dad always says!'

'She is far too chipper for this crazy early hour,' Honey whispered to Pippa.

'We're raring to go!' Danya said with her usual competitive spirit.

'Just wanted to bring you this for the trip,' Ellie said, pulling out a little brown pack with the picture of a Wolf on the front.

'What is it?' Danya asked.

'Whatever it is, I'm not carrying it,' Honey said grumpily. 'My back is about to break!'

'It's one of Dad's survival packs. It's not your run-of-the-mill medical supply bag. There are a few added extras in there. You never know when you might need some dehydrated insect protein to keep energy levels topped up!' Ellie said, grinning, as she walked away.

'Urrgh!' Molly and Honey spat in unison.

'She's kidding, right?' Molly asked.

'Doubt it!' Danya said, tucking the brown bag in between her sleeping bag and backpack.

'Well, I'd rather starve!' Honey said in disgust.

'Sure you would,' Danya giggled. Honey really wasn't cut out for this sort of activity.

'How you feeling this morning, Sal?' Pippa asked, trying to change the subject from dried bugs.

'I'm fine. It's like that song . . . you know . . . whatever will be, will be,' Sally said.

'Never heard of it!' Danya answered.

'Don't forget, Sal. Danya only listens to One Direction these days,' Honey said. 'It's like the rest of her musical education has been completely obliterated since they arrived on the pop scene.'

'Hey!' Danya said, but she couldn't deny it.

'Good attitude Sal! Now then, are we set, Team BFF?' Pippa asked, glancing at Maria. 'That's if I've still got my Team Leader status?'

'Of course . . . *Boss!*' Maria said with a wink. She'd play along until there was a real emergency, then they'd need her to step up to her natural position.

'Team hands!' Pippa called.

'Aaaaaaand *whoooop!*' they all shouted together.

♡

At base camp, Madame Renard stood high on a wooden platform to command the attention of the five schools competing.

'*Bonjour, les filles!*' she called.

'*Bonjour*,' came the surprisingly enthusiastic response, considering how many hours the teams had already been awake.

'Welcome to Chateau Pierre – *La Grande Expedition*! You have done everything possible to prepare for this moment. All that remains is for us to give you one final piece of equipment as you pass under the start banner.'

'Let me guess. A bowling ball for each of us to drag up the mountain . . . just in case we don't have enough to carry!' Maria said, making the L'Etoile girls laugh.

'This is an emergency GPS alarm,' Madame Renard continued. 'The alarm is only to be activated in case of a real emergency, at which point, your precise location will be sent to numerous rescue vehicles dotted along the route. I can assure you that you will never be further than ten minutes away from help.'

She had everyone's full attention.

'That said, I can reassure you that in the five years of running this expedition programme, I have only once seen this device activated. Drink plenty of water, stay focused, and most importantly, help each other. This is about succeeding as a group.'

'Where have we heard that before?' Pippa

whispered to Sally, remembering Madame Ruby's assembly speech.

'*Allez* . . . on my whistle . . .' Madame Renard paused. 'May the best team win! *Un . . . deux . . . trois . . . peeeeeeeeep!*'

'Come on, gang! I told you this was more of a competition than we thought!' Danya said smugly.

'I'm beginning to think she was right,' Honey said to Molly as they raced to keep up. You OK, Moll?'

'As good as I'm going to be in these clodhopper boots! How do I look?' Molly grinned.

'Like the abominable snowman in lipgloss!' Honey replied. 'Come on, or we'll lose them. Some teamwork this is!'

♡

After Team BFF had been walking for about an hour, Sally realised they were completely alone. One by one the other teams had veered off on their own courses.

'Erm . . . is it right that no one else – from twenty-five other teams – is anywhere to be seen?' Sally asked. 'Surely there can't be that many variations of this route?'

'Sugar. She's right!' Honey said, looking around.

The alpine scenery had taken their breath away as

they walked through several pretty villages, feeling the power of the imposing snow-covered peaks above.

'I don't get why we didn't just follow the road like most of the others,' Molly said.

'Well, I didn't like to say, but at least there were people living in those villages. We might even have been able to use a proper toilet!' Honey laughed.

'I'd forgotten about the toilet situation! And I've done nothing but drink water, thanks to Madame R's advice,' Molly said.

'Look,' Danya said, 'while you lot have been yapping, Maria, Pippa and I have been studying our route plan again and we discovered that this track we're on now wasn't on the study maps we originally worked from.'

'Maria and Danya are right,' Pippa said. 'Since we left base camp, we started noticing lots of little *off-piste* tracks leading through the trees and up the mountain and it got us thinking . . .'

'Why should we take the long way around the mountain, when we can head up and over it?' Maria butted in.

Pippa shot her a look.

'Sorry, Pips. Old habits and all that,' Maria said.

'When you said *off-piste,* do you mean we're

following a track which isn't . . . well . . . trackable?'
Molly said. 'GMS!'

GMS = Give me strength, Story Seeker.

'Are you absolutely sure this is a good idea?' Honey
said.

'Think of it as one of our classic L'Etoile adventures!'
Maria said. 'You've never shied away from one of
those before!'

'Erm, I've never been dressed like this before either,'
Molly said, breathing out plumes of freezing fog. 'But
it doesn't mean I'd chose to do it again.'

'Come on,' Pippa said, surprising herself. 'Where's
that Team BFF spirit?'

'OK, OK, but if this goes wrong, you're not coming
to my première, Mimi!' Molly said.

'Deal,' Maria said. 'Let's go.'

So the six girls sang their way as they walked higher
and higher into the Alps.

Team BFF, we're on our way
Hiking is our favourite play
Preparation is a must
We're Team BFF, so eat our dust!

A couple of hours later, Sally suddenly came to an abrupt stop.

'Sorry, guys. I'm calling a break. Pleeease, can we stop for some lunch? My stomach is rumbling like a freight train.'

Maria checked her watch. 'One-thirty. Goodness, doesn't time fly when you're having fun?'

'OK, Team BFF. Let's see what sort of a lunch Chateau Pierre has packed for us. Honey – I think it's in your rucksack,' Danya said.

The girls couldn't hide their disappointment at the dried out cheese and ham baguette, bag of ready-salted crisps and carton of *jus de pommes*.

Jus de pommes = apple juice, Story-seeker.

'Whatever happened to energy food?' Maria exclaimed. 'This is going top of my complaints list in my feedback report for Chateau Pierre.'

'We have to do a feedback report?' Honey asked.

'Of course we don't. It's Maria's thing. She blogs about everything after the fact to give her invaluable opinion and improvement suggestions,' Molly replied, with a laugh.

'You crack me up, Maria,' Honey said.

'I know – only Maria Fitzfoster could be at her happiest when creating extra hassle for herself,' Pippa said.

'What? It's crucial to get feedback on all things! Imagine when the fifth-years are sitting here, in exactly this position, at exactly this moment, unpacking a steaming, pre-cooked, pre-packed, flavoursome carbonara pasta,' Maria said.

'Oh, don't!' Sally said. 'I can almost taste it!'

'Well, there are always Wolfette's dehydrated scorpions if we need a little pick me up!' Pippa giggled.

'Now I'm going to be sick!' Honey said, clutching her mouth.

'Shhhh . . . do you hear that?' Danya said, jumping up. 'Quick, behind this tree, everyone. We don't want whoever it is to follow our new clever route!'

'The food bag!' Molly whispered, just in time for Pippa to whisk it out of sight.

♡

We're the team from Lakewood High
The only team who'll make you cry

We mean business when we say
Other teams, get out the way!

Team BFF held their breath as a Lakewood High team came into view.

'Ahhhh, I love a good sing-song in the mountain air. Just a shame some of us are tone deaf,' the first girl, who they recognised as Philly Malby, drawled, as she sat on the very log where Team BFF had been lunching only moments earlier.

The other girls followed, sniggering.

'Get a move on, Hollywood, I'm dying of thirst over here!' Philly screeched.

Team BFF followed Philly's gaze and gasped as another girl entered the clearing. She dropped to her knees and shuffled off her enormous backpack. As she fumbled for the zip, her big hood dropped back to her shoulders, exposing a sweaty, but unmistakeably familiar face.

The L'Etoile girls could barely silence their own gasps.

'I . . . I . . . told you!' Sally whispered. 'I knew it . . . I . . .'

'Shhhh!' Pippa warned in her quietest voice. 'You'll give us away!'

Pippa wasn't entirely sure why they were hiding in the first place. They had every right to be there, but it was a bit late to walk out now. It would look weird.

'Who gave you the right to be on Team Dynamo anyways?' came a familiar American voice.

'We were the only team of five with a space for one more, Philly. Don't you remember?' said the red-headed girl called Kate.

'I'm ... sorry,' Lucinda said, completely out of breath.

'Has she been carrying two rucksacks all this time!' Molly whispered to Honey, noticing two lying on the ground around her.

'You're right! That's got to be illegal,' Honey mumbled back.

'No need to be sorry ...' Philly said. 'Just useful.'

Lucinda nodded.

'Get the lunch out, then, Hollywood!' Kate said.

'Oh, have I got it? Yes . . . right,' Lucinda said, quickly searching through her bags.

Pippa couldn't bear to watch any more so took the Team Leader decision for them to move on, quickly, quietly and unseen. The others were only too happy to follow. They had so much to talk about!

11

Crossing A Line

'I just can't believe Lucifette is here,' Molly said. 'I mean, I know you said you thought she was, Sally, but I don't think I ever really believed it was possible!'

'Hoped it wasn't, more like!' Pippa said with a shudder.

'I'm not crazy,' Sally said. 'I know what I saw.'

'Oh, I know, and I didn't mean to doubt you, it's just WATC of her being on the same mountain at the same time, within the same ten metre radius of us?' Molly said, wiping her brow.

'The question is, what are we going to do about it?' Maria said, the old hatred bubbling up inside her.

'I'm a bit annoyed we felt the need to hide. If we'd

just stayed where we were and continued with our rubbish lunch, it would all be out in the open by now. No need for all this secrecy and anxiety,' Pippa said.

'You're right! Why did we scamper into the bushes like escaped convicts?' Maria said.

Danya and Honey had been awfully quiet since the episode in the clearing.

'It was all bit too awful for words, wasn't it?' Honey said eventually.

'And you don't know half the things that girl has done!' Sally said.

'You're right. I can't even begin to imagine. I bet Philly is capable of all sorts of nastiness,' Honey continued.

'Not Philly! Who cares about her! I mean Lucifette. Lucinda Marciano, the girl who has made the last ten years of my life a misery,' Sally snapped.

'Oh, sorry, Sally.' Danya came to Honey's rescue. 'Honey didn't mean anything by it. We know you've been to hell and back with that girl. It's just that she looks like she's getting her comeuppance now, and I guess we're just not used to seeing girls treating other girls so spitefully.'

'Is that . . . OMG, it so is!' Molly said, finding new strength in her limbs as she saw the Chateau Pierre flag up ahead.

'We made it!!' Danya and Honey squealed together.

'I've never been so happy to see a campsite in all my days!' Maria said.

'Well done, Team BFF!' Pippa said. 'I'm proud of all of you.'

'Thanks, Boss!' Danya said.

'By the looks of things, we're the first ones to make it!' Maria said with glee, noticing how silent the camp was.

'Hey, you!' came a furious shout from the mountain behind.

Danya swung round to see Philly making a beeline for them.

'Are you talking to us?' Maria said.

What was it about confrontation that gave Maria such strength and . . . well, crazy confidence, Story-seeker?

Sally rolled her eyes. 'I might have remembered we always seem to sniff out trouble!'

'Yeah, I'm talking to you . . . all of you. Today, you got lucky. Today, we gave you a chance. Tomorrow, we go to war!' Philly said. And, without waiting for an answer, or indeed the rest of her team mates to appear, she made off towards the Lakewood site.

'We got lucky?' Danya cried.

'Gave us a chance?' Maria spat. 'Who does she think she's talking to?'

'Girls, come on. Let's not stoop to her level and ruin the moment,' Pippa said. 'Let's get our tents up and some hot food in our bellies before we all pass out.'

'Spoken like a true team leader,' Molly said. 'Let's go, guys.'

And with that, Team BFF found the L'Etoile site, to discover just how good Pippa was at pitching tents with her eyes shut!

'Team BFF! Wow! You must have rocketed over that mountain to get here so fast,' a breathless Ellie exclaimed as she and Belle's Beagles arrived. 'I thought we had this in the bag!'

'HA! Not sure how we did it really,' Pippa said.

'Did you find a route up and over the mountain rather than round?' Ellie asked. 'Genius! Risky . . . but genius!'

'That's Team BFF for you,' Maria said with a wink. 'Risky but genius.'

'Come on, Ellie,' Belle called over, struggling with her tent. 'We're all starving and you're the one with the stove!'

'Coming . . .' she called back. 'Catch you later, girls.' And she sprinted over to join the rest of her team.

♡

'Amazing sausage casserole!' Molly said, mopping her bowl dry with a hunk of French bread.

'I feel like I'm about to go into a food coma and never wake up,' Honey said, settling down into her sleeping bag.

'Good cooking skills, Team Leader,' Molly said to Pippa.

'Why, thank you,' Pippa said. 'Glad you approve – although expect the same thing tomorrow. Unfortunately that's the only thing Uncle Harry taught me to cook on a camping stove apart from a tin of baked beans.'

'Nothing wrong with a tin of baked beans,' Danya said. 'In fact, I've burned off so much energy today, I think I'd eat an entire tin now if we had any.'

'You all right, Sally? You've barely said a word since we got here,' Molly said.

'Actually, no,' Sally said, unzipping her sleeping bag. 'Not really. I know you'll think I'm being ridiculous, given what a misery Lucinda made my and all of our lives, but now I've had time to think, I can't help feeling a bit sorry for her.'

'Sally!' Pippa said in surprise, trying not to let on

that she'd been battling with her own feelings of guilt about Lucinda's predicament.

'Yes,' Sally said. 'Do you think we should have helped her? Last night by the coach, and earlier?'

'And what would happen once we rescue her? Not that I feel much like rescuing her. We can't protect her beyond the weekend,' Maria said. 'She has to stand up for herself. She didn't seem to have a problem at L'Etoile!'

'Ooooh, I don't know,' Molly groaned. 'I'd be lying if I didn't feel some sort obligation to step in and help her.'

'Well, look. Seeing as Honey and I don't have any history with Lucifette, how about we make the call on this? Let's not worry about the past and what we should or shouldn't have done. How about we start fresh tomorrow, and if we see anything mean happening, we step in?' Danya said.

The girls nodded.

Only Sally sat motionless.

'No,' she said finally.

'No?' everyone asked.

'No, not tomorrow. I need to see Lucinda now. To check she's OK. I can't sleep until I know,' Sally said.

'I'll come with you,' Pippa said. 'I spotted the Lakewood camp when I went for water earlier.'

'Should we all—' Molly started.

'No,' Maria said. 'I think it's better if it's just Pippa and Sally. Too many of us will draw attention.'

'And intimidate the life out of Lucifette!' Molly said. 'Don't forget she still hasn't got a clue we're even here yet.'

'Let's call her Lucinda from now on, shall we?' Sally said. 'That's a good place to start.'

Even though the majority of the group couldn't quite believe they were agreeing to help their arch-enemy, they nodded and Pippa unzipped their tent to check the coast was clear.

'Wait!' Maria shouted, grabbing her rucksack. 'Take this!'

'You brought walkie-talkies all the way out here? I'm beginning to think you love them more than me!' Molly said with a giggle.

'You take one – keep it on channel two and have it on in your coat pocket so we can hear everything Lucifet . . . Lucinda says,' Maria said, ignoring her sister.

'OK, good. Wish us luck!' Sally said.

'Good luck!'

12

The Leopard Who Changed Her Spots

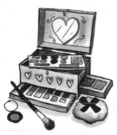

'You're absolutely sure that's Lucinda's tent?' Sally asked Pippa, squinting at a lone little one-man tent pitched slightly away from the main Lakewood camp.

'As sure as I can be. Look – aren't they the gloves she was wearing?' Pippa said, pointing at some red-and-white ski gloves sticking out from a pair of walking boots.

Sally gasped. They were Lucinda's all right. She had been with her when she'd bought them during a ski trip to Whistler with their American school.

'Aren't we going to scare the living daylights out of her, if we just start unzipping the door?'

Sally said. 'We don't even know if she's in there!'

'Have you ever been camping before? Tent walls aren't made of stone you know,' Pippa said. 'Go over and whisper something through the canvas. Something only you could know about her so she'll know it's you.'

'Good idea. The gloves should be enough,' Sally said, creeping towards the tent. Then, taking one last look at Pippa for encouragement, she whispered, 'Lucinda!'

'Who's there?' came a small voice.

'Lucinda – it's me . . . Sally. Sally Sudbury. I see you're still wearing your red Whistler gloves,' Sally said.

The door to the tent unzipped and Lucinda's tear-stained face popped out, a picture of disbelief and elation.

'Oh, my goodness, Sally, is it really you? Come in, come in!' Lucinda said. She'd known there were some L'Etoile students competing at Chateau Pierre, but given her history and reputation at the school, she'd kept her head down. She hadn't realised it was her old year group.

'I've got Pippa with me,' Sally said, nodding over to where Pippa was hiding.

'Pippa! Wow! Tell her to come too. Quick, before the others see!' Lucinda said, beckoning her.

As the girls sat together in the torchlight, they didn't speak. They just stared at one another, unable to find the words.

'Well, this is weird,' Pippa said, breaking the ice. 'What—'

'Lucinda, I . . .' Sally started to speak but Lucinda put up a hand.

'Hold on, Sally . . . before you say anything, please can I? I feel I owe you both that much,' Lucinda said. 'I never thought I'd get the chance, and yet here you are, here you both are.'

Her face flushed with joy as she paused again to look at Sally and Pippa, who proceeded to watch the fearsome, horrible girl they'd once known pour out her regrets for all the bad she'd done and beg their forgiveness.

'I just hope that one day, when we're old and grey, we might look back on this moment as a new beginning, Sally,' Lucinda said, her eyes searching Sally's for a hint of support. 'And you, Pippa.'

Sally glanced at Pippa who gave a half-smile. She desperately wanted to believe this new, gushing Lucinda, but it was difficult to forget so much hurt and upset. It would take time. For the moment, though, they were both content to give Lucinda the chance to make amends.

'Lucinda,' Sally said. 'Thanks for everything you've said. If I'm honest I've dreamed of the day where you would finally realise how awful you've been and apologise, but I never imagined it would come. I'm sure I speak for all the girls, it's hard to take in your apology fully, but I feel like this is a start. Life is too short to make forever enemies.'

'I completely agree. I know it's a big ask. I was a complete horror and I don't even have an excuse,' Lucinda said.

'I'd say karma has turned the tables on you, having seen the way those awful Lakewood girls are with you,' Pippa said. 'No one should have to go through that . . . not even—'

'Me? You're probably right. I deserve everything I get. But how have you seen any of that stuff? I didn't even know you guys were here until just now,' Lucinda said.

'We'd just arrived when we saw that hideous Philly bullying you in the car park . . . and we saw the way they make you carry all the stuff,' Sally said, feeling ashamed all over again for not having helped. 'Look, none of us are completely faultless, but we're here now and we'd like to help you.'

'If you want us to,' Pippa added tentatively.

'You'd help me? After everything I've done?' Lucinda said, her eyes pricking with tears.

'Absolutely. If the last few years have taught me anything, it's that life is for living and for forgiving and . . . well, if you're prepared to try, then we are too. Right, Pips?' Sally said.

'Right,' Pippa said.

Lucinda was stunned. She didn't deserve these girls. Not after she'd made their lives such a misery in the past few years. She'd have to prove to them that her friendship was worth it. 'Thanks so much, guys,' she said.

'Now what about this Lakewood lot?' Sally said.

'Arrrrgh, hold on! The walkie-talkie! I completely forgot. The others will be going crazy wondering what's happening!' Pippa said.

'One of Maria's gadgets?' Lucinda grinned. Just talking about these old, familiar faces warmed her heart.

'Erm . . . yes. They wanted to listen in. Do you mind?' Sally answered.

'Not at all,' Lucinda said.

'TESTING . . .TESTING . . . ARE YOU RECEIVING? OVER,' Pippa said.

'YOU'RE ABOUT HALF AN HOUR LATE . . . BUT RECEIVING . . . OVER!' Maria snapped.

'She's annoyed!' Pippa said, with a slight smile. It felt good to be calling the shots.

'GUYS . . . SALLY HERE . . .'

'SALLY! NEVER SAY YOUR NAME . . . IN CASE SOMEONE'S LISTENING IN . . . OVER,' Danya said angrily. Had Maria not taught them anything?

'Who's that?' Lucinda whispered, realising that was a voice she didn't know.

'Danya Sawyer . . . one of the new twins,' Sally whispered back.

'Wow,' Lucinda said, thinking how the old her would have had riots with two sets of twins.

'OK, OK . . . SORRY . . . FORGOT TO SWITCH ON WALKIE-TALKIE,' Sally said. 'ALL GOOD HERE. ABOUT TO RUN THROUGH LAKEWOOD PROBLEM SO THOUGHT YOU MIGHT WANT TO LISTEN IN . . . OVER.'

'ALL EARS . . . OVER,' Danya answered.

'May I?' Lucinda said quietly to Pippa and Sally. This was her chance to build some serious bridges with her old L'Etoile adversaries.

'Sure!' Sally said.

'ERM . . . LUCINDA HERE . . . I'M SO, SO SORRY . . . FOR EVERYTHING . . . AND I KNOW YOUR GUT INSTINCT WILL BE TO DISTRUST ME, BUT I NEED TO TELL YOU SOMETHING IMPORTANT TO HELP YOU WIN THE EXPEDITION . . . OVER,' Lucinda babbled into the radio.

Maria and Molly Fitzfoster's mouths fell open.

What? They mouthed at each other incredulously. Who was this girl and what had she done with evil Lucinda?

'ERM . . . HI LUCINDA . . .' Molly began, realising Maria was too shocked to speak. 'WE'RE LISTENING . . . OVER.'

'OK, GREAT . . .' Lucinda glanced at Sally and Pippa for their approval to continue.

'Go ahead,' Sally said. She had absolutely no idea what Lucinda was about to say. She thought they were here to help her fight off the Lakewood girls but now it seemed that Lucinda was the one offering them help!

 105 ♥

'HI, LUCINDA. WE HAVEN'T MET . . . THIS IS DANYA SAWYER,' Danya said, before she was interrupted by Maria.

'SHE'S A GENIUS, BTW . . .'

BTW = By the Way, Story-seeker.

Danya smiled.

'HI, DANYA,' Lucinda said.

'CAN YOU TELL US ANY MORE? HOW ARE THEY PLANNING ON BEATING US?' Danya asked.

'TEAM DYNAMO ARE COMPLETE CHEATS. THEY HAVEN'T GOT AN ORIENTEERING BONE IN THEIR BODIES. THEY WOULDN'T KNOW HOW TO PLAN A ROUTE IF THEIR LIVES DEPENDED ON IT,' Lucinda said. 'THEY'VE BEEN WATCHING YOU GUYS SINCE YOU ARRIVED. OF COURSE THEY HAD NO ACCESS TO YOU OR YOUR PLANS BEFORE WE GOT TO CHATEAU PIERRE, BUT AS SOON AS THEY WERE ABLE, THEY'VE BEEN ON YOUR TAIL . . .'

'What do you mean on our tail?' Pippa whispered,

even more quietly than before, glancing behind her at the tent door.

'THEY'VE TAKEN IT IN TURNS TO EAVESDROP ON YOU WHEREVER POSSIBLE – THE CANTEEN, THE SHOWERS, EVEN THE TOILETS. AND WHILE YOU WERE ALL AT BREAKFAST THIS MORNING, KATE SNUCK INTO YOUR ROOM TO FIND YOUR ROUTE PLAN AND PHOTOGRAPH IT,' Lucinda continued.

'THEY DID WHAT?' Maria exploded.

'AND SHE GOT IT, TOO, NOT THAT IT WAS MUCH USE . . . YOU ALL ENDED UP GOING OFF-PISTE ANYWAY SO WE LOST YOU. IF YOU'D HAVE FOLLOWED YOUR EXACT PLANNED ROUTE ALL THE WAY, WE'D HAVE MADE A RUN FOR THE FINISH LINE IN THE LAST MINUTE, TAKING YOU COMPLETELY BY SURPRISE,' Lucinda explained.

'I can't believe this, can you?' Molly whispered to Honey.

'I know! We can't even have a weekend camping without trouble following us up a mountain!' Honey answered.

'HOW DID THEY END UP TAKING THE SAME OFF-PISTE TRACK AS US THEN, IF WE TOOK A DETOUR?' Danya asked.

'Good point!' Maria mouthed.

'WE WERE FOLLOWING YOU AT THAT POINT WHEN WE SAW YOU VEER OFF UP THE MOUNTAIN. OF COURSE THEN OUR ONLY OPTION WAS TO TRY AND KEEP UP AND HOPE TO OVERTAKE YOU RIGHT AT THE END, BUT WE HAD TO KEEP ENOUGH OF A SAFE DISTANCE SO YOU WOULDN'T SPOT US. WE COULD NEVER HAVE EXPLAINED AWAY THE COINCIDENCE OF US PICKING THE SAME TRACK YOU DID OUT OF ALL THE ONES WE PASSED, WITHOUT YOU REALISING WE WERE CHEATING YOU.'

Maria gasped. 'AND THEN YOU LOST US AROUND LUNCHTIME . . .'

'YES! PHILLY WAS FURIOUS. I THOUGHT SHE WAS GOING TO PUSH US ALL DOWN THE MOUNTAIN. BUT HOW DID YOU KNOW THAT?' Lucinda asked.

'BECAUSE WE HEARD YOU COMING. YOU WEREN'T AS INVISIBLE AS YOU

THOUGHT. WE AUTOMATICALLY HID
FROM SIGHT – PARTLY BECAUSE WE
RECOGNISED PHILLY'S VOICE COMING
THROUGH THE TREES AND WANTED
TO SEE FROM AFAR WHETHER *YOU*
WERE WITH THEM . . .'

'I SEE . . .' Lucinda said, feeling sad that the girls
had seen her in one of her darkest moments and not
helped her. 'CAN'T BLAME YOU FOR NOT
ANNOUNCING YOURSELVES.'

'NO . . . YOU CAN'T,' Maria snapped. 'AND
HOW DO WE KNOW YOU HAVEN'T
SENT SOME SORT OF A SIGNAL TO
SET US UP AGAIN AND THAT PHILLY
ISN'T STANDING OUTSIDE YOUR TENT
LISTENING TO EVERYTHING RIGHT
NOW?'

'She isn't, honestly. They've all gone to the
Lakewood campfire to toast marshmallows. Philly
said if I dare show my face, she'd empty a load of
insects into my tent when I'm asleep tonight,' Lucinda
said, her face pale.

'MARIA, MOLLY, DANYA, HONEY,'
Sally said. 'PLEASE TRUST ME ON THIS.
LUCINDA DESERVES A CHANCE TO

MAKE THINGS RIGHT. WE'VE ALL HAD A SECOND CHANCE AT SOME POINT,' Sally said.

'I AGREE,' Pippa said. 'IT'S TIME TO WIPE THE SLATE CLEAN AND HELP EACH OTHER GET THROUGH THIS.'

'OK, OK,' Maria conceded. Was this all for real? Were they all on the same team?

'SO WHAT'S THE PLAN FOR TOMORROW, LUCINDA?' Pippa said, taking over as leader. 'THEY KNOW NOW THEY CAN'T RELY ON US TO STICK TO THE ROUTE.'

'SAME PLAN AS YESTERDAY. BUT TO FOLLOW A BIT MORE CLOSELY AND AVOID LOSING YOU THIS TIME. IT'S D-DAY TOMORROW AND PHILLY'S ON A MISSION TO COME OUT ON TOP!' Lucinda said.

'YEAH? WELL, SO ARE WE!' Maria exclaimed. 'COME BACK, GIRLS. WE NEED TO TALK TACTICS . . . BUT LEAVE THAT WALKIE-TALKIE WITH LUCINDA IN CASE WE HAVE TO CONTACT HER.'

'REALLY?' Lucinda blushed. 'THANKS

AGAIN, ALL OF YOU. I WON'T LET YOU DOWN.'

And with that, Sally and Pippa snuck off back to Camp L'Etoile for a full dissection of the evening's events!

13

How to Outfox the Fox!

'I just can't believe it!' Pippa exclaimed. 'If you'd told me a year ago that I'd be sitting in a tent with Lucinda Marciano, offering her our help and friendship, I'd have said you were insane!'

'And you're sure she's for real?' Maria said, who was still finding it hard to trust her.

And let's face it, Story-seeker. Who wouldn't, given Lucinda's track record for wickedness?

'You didn't see her face when we turned up,' Sally said. 'It was like someone turned a light on in her eyes.

Not even *you* could have put on a performance like that, Moll.'

'And let's not forget, it was us who approached her,' Danya said. 'I can see why we'd need to be suspicious if she'd come to us out of the blue, but she didn't.'

'Plus, everything she said makes complete sense,' Pippa said. 'We wouldn't have noticed anyone we didn't know hanging around listening to our conversations back at the chateau – particularly if they kept changing who it was. It was quite natural other people would be around.'

'Pippa's right,' Danya said. 'They had the advantage over us from the very start. Lucinda only had to give our names for them to Google what we look like and spy on us without any trouble. I wouldn't recognise anyone from Team Dynamo other than Lucinda, Philly and Kate, would you?'

'Nope,' Maria said.

'So that's how they've managed to spy on us without us noticing!' Pippa said.

'What are we going to do tomorrow?' Honey said. 'We can't stop them from following us. Not without exposing Lucinda's betrayal of them. I don't think she'd survive the fall-out from that!'

'I might have a plan,' Maria said.

'And that's why we love you!' Molly said, giving her sister a squeeze.

'The simplest way to beat them is to play them at their own game. They want to follow us? Then we'll lead them. Right up the *mountain* path!' Maria said.

'I hope you're going to give us bit more of an explanation than that!' Pippa said.

'Yes, please. I can't face one of your usual "cards close to your chest" cliffhangers,' Sally said. 'I don't think my nerves could take that this weekend.'

'Would I do that to you?' Maria asked with a wink.

'YES!' the others exclaimed.

'Tell you what. I'll trade crucial info for a hot chocolate. Deal?' Maria said.

'You talk, I'll boil!' Molly said, whizzing outside to put some water on the little camping stove.

'OK,' Maria said, a couple of minutes later. 'The only way I can see to play this is to make sure Team Dynamo keep up with us, then right at the end we'll give them the slip and sprint to victory, while they're left wondering how quickly a rescue vehicle might get to them!'

Maria spread the Parc du Mercantour map in front of them.

'What's that X for?' Danya asked, noticing where Maria had marked up.

'That is what we're going to call *Loser Point*!'

'Is that a river?' Honey asked, seeing where a long line of blue ran right through the cross.

'Yes,' Maria answered excitedly.

'But that river literally divides the mountain in half!' Molly exclaimed. 'How on earth are we going to cross it? I can't see any bridge symbols anywhere. I knew there was a reason for not going *off-piste!*'

'No, no bridges. Which is why every other team will be crossing it using the main road, which has been built over it . . . see . . . there,' Maria said, pointing to a village halfway down the mountain.

'So how are *we* going to do it? And don't tell me you happen to have a wild water rapid dingy in that rucksack!' Sally said.

'Ha! No. But this is where it becomes a leap of faith and part of the reason I never usually share my plans with you lot is that there is always a – shall we say – *unsure* part of my plan.'

'Now she tells us!' Honey said, rolling her eyes.

'And like this time, the unsure part is usually the bit our success hinges on,' Maria said, wondering whether she should have kept it to herself after all.

'God help us!' Molly groaned.

'Have I ever let you down before?' Maria asked.

'We've come close a few times, but no,' Molly answered.

'Then just hear me out. See here, where it says *Table Vert*?' Maria pointed to a name just above the cross she'd drawn. 'I'm pretty sure there's a natural stone shelf stretching all the way across the river which you can walk over without even getting your boots wet!'

The group sat in silence, contemplating how on earth Maria would know something like that.

'How can you tell *that* from looking at *this*?' Molly said, incredulous.

'Research!' Maria exclaimed. 'After Madame Ruby told us we were coming to Parc du Mercantour, Dan and I immediately hit the Internet to see if there was anything which might help us plan our route, and that's when I found a load of photos of people walking across this stone ridge.'

'Yes, yes! I remember those pictures,' Danya said excitedly. 'But I don't remember seeing a location name. How do we know those were pictures of *Table Vert*?'

'We don't for sure . . . and that's the leap of faith. But I'm eighty per cent certain,' Maria said.

'Oh, I don't know about this, Mimi,' Molly said. 'If we can't cross at that point, we'll be completely stuck, and by the time we've walked all the way back down the mountain to the village road, not only will we not have won, we'll be last!'

'And it will be right at the end of the day when it's starting to get dark,' Danya said, spotting the finish line on the other side of the river and figuring it would take them until at least dusk to reach that point.

'How can we stop Team Dynamo from just following us over if they're hot on our tail?' Sally asked.

'Molly will fake an injury,' Maria said, grinning at her actor sister. 'Something which prevents her and us from being able to continue, but this will take place just before the crossing. Once Team Dynamo realise something's wrong, it's my bet that Philly won't want to stop if she thinks we're out of the race, and they will have no choice but to navigate their own way to the finish line. Their natural option will be to go south, towards the road, once they figure out they can't cross and think we've got it wrong.'

'And as soon as they pass us we'll head straight up to *Table Vert* and win!' Danya cried. 'You are brilliant, Maria Fitzfoster!'

Maria smiled as humbly as she could manage.

'I don't know how you think these things up!' Honey said.

'OK, I'm in,' Sally said thoughtfully. 'Even if *Table Vert* ends up not being a crossing at all, it's still worth taking the risk. We might not win, but Team Dynamo won't either and that's all I care about.'

'So we're in agreement then?' Maria said.

'Yep!' came the response.

'Right, then. Drink up and let's get some sleep. It's already so late and we're going to need all our wits about us to outfox the Mean Team tomorrow,' Pippa said.

'If they're the Mean Team, does that make us the Dream Team?' Molly said.

'Always!' Pippa winked. 'Night, BFFs.'

14

La Grande Expedition: Day Two

'Hey, BFFs!' came a shout from the trees. 'Wait up!'

Ellie was running towards them with Belle and the other Beagles close behind.

'Ready for day two?' Ellie called. 'We're going to do our best to beat you girls, but I have a feeling it will just be my old cronies, Lakewood High, giving you a run for your money.'

'Don't let Belle hear you say that! Good luck, Beagles!' Danya said, but before she could say anything further, Ellie had bolted off towards the starting line.

'Wow. Wolfette means business!' Molly said to Belle.

'She does today,' Belle said. 'She's chomping at the bit after our disastrous day yesterday.'

'Why? What happened?' Maria asked. 'We thought Wolfette would have had you drilling a tunnel through the mountain or something with all her survival experience!'

'Hmmm. Unfortunately she didn't get chance to be brilliant,' Belle answered. 'You might have noticed, we're a girl down . . .'

'Oh, yes! Where's Alice?' Molly said suddenly. 'Is she OK?'

'Not really, no. Everything was going great, but about four miles into the route, Alice came down with the most horrendous bout of food poisoning – or at least that's what we thought it was. We activated the GPS alarm and by the time the emergency services got to us, they whisked her off with a suspected appendicitis!' Belle said.

'The poor thing. Where is she now?' Honey said.

'In some French hospital having an operation. Her family flew over, so they're with her. I just can't believe the timing of it. An illness like that is a nightmare at any time, let alone being struck down when you're halfway up a mountain!' Belle said.

'It's terrible. I hope she's all right,' Pippa said. 'What

have you guys decided to do? Go on today, just the five of you?'

'Ellie's still hoping we're in with a chance and I haven't the heart to tell her the rest of the Beagles' hearts just aren't in it. It was all a bit draining and stressful yesterday,' Belle said.

'Let's go Beagles! PMA! PMA!' Ellie called out, quoting her father's catchphrase.

PMA = Positive mental attitude, Story-seeker.

'I'd better go, or she'll explode!' Belle said. 'Good luck guys – win it for L'Etoile!'

'We'll do our best!' Maria promised.

'Oh, and by the way,' Belle swung back around. 'I nearly forgot to say. Did you know Lucifette's here ... with Lakewood High?'

'Really?'

'No way!'

'Is she?'

'Wow!'

Team BFF's exclamations came a bit too quickly and with not a single expression of genuine surprise on any of their faces.

Belle looked at them quizzically.

'If I didn't know better, Team BFF, I'd say I haven't told you anything you didn't already know and that, true to form, you are up to something!'

'See you at the finish line,' Pippa said with a grin.

'Not if my Beagles see you first! PMA, Team BFF!' Belle smiled and ran off to join Ellie and the others.

♡

'Does Lucinda know anything about today's plan?' Molly whispered to Maria, as they waited for Madame Renard's starting whistle.

'I didn't want to burden her with knowing too much,' Maria said. 'I radioed her this morning only to say that we were going to let them follow us, but when she and her team realise something's happened to Team BFF, she's to encourage them down the mountain, not up!' Maria said.

'And she didn't ask why?' Molly said.

'Nope,' Maria answered.

'It's nice when people surprise you, isn't it, Mimi?' Molly said, always intent on seeing the good in everyone.

'Let's just say people rarely surprise me,' Maria said. 'I'm just praying this is one of those times!'

♡

The first part of the expedition flew by. The game of cat and mouse that Team Dynamo and Team BFF were involved in kept them both amused – mainly because each team believed they were the cat!

'Do they really think we can't see them zigzagging from one "hiding place" to another?' Danya whispered to Maria.

'I know, right? Those electric-blue Lakewood jackets are hardly alpine camouflage, are they?' Maria said.

'How much further before we reach the river? I think my blisters are getting blisters!' Sally groaned.

'Danya reckons about another two miles,' Maria said. 'That's right isn't it, Dan?'

'Yes . . . at best,' Danya said.

'Do you want to stop for a bit, Sal?' Pippa said. She had given up trying to be Team Leader today. Maria and Danya were on a mission and it would have been useless to try and take over.

'I'd love to stop – for good! But I'll be OK. The longer we take, the longer poor Lucinda has to carry all that stuff for those horrible girls. Let's keep going,' Sally said, taking a swig of water.

'Thinking about it, it's wrong of the teachers at Lakewood to have ever let Lucinda be in Philly's group when she's so awful to her,' Molly said.

'I know,' Sally said, knowing more than most what it felt like for no one to notice somebody suffering. Before she'd arrived at L'Etoile no one seemed to notice what she went through with Lucinda.

'Have you thought about what injury you're going to sustain, Molly?' Honey asked, trying to change the subject.

'It's between taking an "actor's tumble" and breaking my leg . . . or I could go the whole hog and you guys could lift one of these fallen tree branches up and place it strategically across me so there's no real weight crushing me, but it looks like I'm in real trouble,' Molly said, feeling pleased with herself.

Molly Fitzfoster loves a wind up, Story-seeker. This sort of role-play is very her and Maria. They've done it ever since they were children and have become excellent at fooling everyone.

'Ooooh, the second one,' Honey said.

'Let's see what props are on-hand once we get to the

river, shall we?' Maria said. 'We aren't going to have that long to set this little accident up.'

'I wonder what they'll do when they realise we've stopped,' Molly said. 'If they don't come running to help when they hear me wailing in pain, they truly are evil!'

'Only one way to find out. Let's get moving!' Pippa said, before launching into song.

Team BFF, we're on our way
Hiking is our favourite play
Preparation is a must
We're Team BFF, you'll eat our dust!

♡

'Shhhh!' Maria said suddenly. 'Stop singing – listen!'

Team BFF immediately fell silent, having sung their way through the last couple of miles.

'Do you hear that?' Maria said again.

'The river!' Molly squealed. 'I can hear the river!'

'It sounds like it's running really fast!' Honey said, slightly afraid.

'Don't worry, Honey. Where we're going to cross, we'll hardly get wet at all,' Danya reassured her sister.

'We hope!' Maria said, secretly terrified of the Table Vert picture she'd seen all those weeks ago of hikers crossing on a natural stone ledge.

'Quick, girls – help me move this,' Molly said, spotting a fallen tree not far from where they were standing.

'What a spot of luck!' Maria said, hoping that it was a good sign.

'It's perfect!' Molly said. 'It's still half in the ground so that's taking most of the weight. If we can prop up the other end a bit, it will look like I'm being crushed, but really it'll hardly be touching me. We'll just have to rely on Philly's lot not looking too closely . . . but I shouldn't imagine that will be an issue!'

'You're going to freeze on that icy ground!' Honey said. Here – put my jacket under you.'

'No, thanks, Honey,' Molly said. 'I would if I thought they wouldn't see it sticking out underneath me. We'd have difficulty explaining how I had time to make sure I had a comfy landing yet no time to avoid a falling tree!'

'D'oh! You're right,' Honey said.

'Ready?' Maria said, as she, Pippa and Danya prepared to lift the top end of the fallen tree up off the ground so Molly could take her place underneath.

'Yep!' Molly said, adrenalin pumping.

'One, two, three, go!' Maria said.

The girls heaved, and Molly, having ruffled up her hair and smudged her lipgloss across her face for a more panic-stricken look, quickly slid underneath, while Sally and Honey slid a couple of other branches in next to her to raise the trunk up a bit.

'OK, done. You can let go, guys,' Honey said, giving Molly a smile.

'Sure?' Danya and Maria said. 'We're not about to crush her for real, are we?'

'No,' Sally said. 'Honey and I have packed it out really well around her.'

'All right. Let go, everyone,' Maria instructed as the girls removed their hold on the enormous log.

They all held their breath for a second.

'You OK, Moll?' Maria said.

'Happy as Larry!' Molly said with a giggle. 'How do I look?'

'In real trouble!!' Danya said.

'Can you twist one of your legs a bit so it looks like you've broken it?' Maria said.

'She's not a contortionist!' Sally exclaimed.

'Like this?' Molly said, bending one leg at the knee so it looked as if it had been stuck on backwards.

'Oh my god! You are a contortionist! How is that even possible?' Danya said, grimacing.

'Double-jointed!' Molly grinned.

'Perfect, Moll!' Maria said proudly. 'Right, I reckon they've stopped to see exactly where we are on the map. We passed a named track back there which will give them our location near the river so they'll think we've hit a dead end and stopped.'

'Just let me know when to begin,' Molly said, pumped and ready for her director to call 'Action'!

'Maybe we should start singing again, to give the impression we're on the move, then when we stop, that's when you can start wailing, Molly,' Maria said.

'Good idea. When they get here and see what's happened they'll assume the tree fell while we were singing so they didn't hear it happen.'

'OK, here goes!' Pippa said.

Team BFF, we're on our way
Hiking is our favourite play
Preparation is a must
We're Team BFF, so eat our dust!

'Aaaaaaaaaarrrrrrrrrrrgggghhhhhhh!' Molly screamed at the top of her lungs.

'MOOOOLLLLLY!! NO!' Maria shouted, getting into character.

'HELP!' Honey called. 'SOMEONE HELP US, PLEASE!'

'More, Moll, more!' Maria whispered. 'I don't see them coming yet!'

'Arrrrrrggggggggghhhh!' Molly screamed again, several times.

'I see them, I see them!' Danya said. 'They're coming . . . about thirty seconds away.'

'Keep going, Molly,' Maria said. 'It's show-time!'

15

A Really Bad Feeling Saves The Day

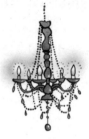

Having heard running water up ahead, Team Dynamo had been pouring over their map to try and work out where on earth they were, when they heard a blood-curdling scream coming from Team BFF.

'What was that?' Philly shouted.

The girls stood silently listening to what sounded like a wild animal being murdered.

'Something really bad has happened!' Kate said. 'What should we do?'

'Do?' Philly said coldly. 'We go take a look. These L'Etoilettes have led us a right song and dance and they're paying for it.'

'But I think someone's been really hurt,' Lucinda said quietly, immediately recognising a Molly Fitzfoster performance from her stunts in the Ivy Room at L'Etoile over the years.

'And what do you suppose we do about it?' Philly barked.

'We should go and help them,' Lucinda said, knowing that whatever she suggested, Philly Malby would do exactly the opposite.

'What – and forfeit the race? I don't think so, Hollywood!' Philly said. 'Everyone, get moving. We need to get the rest of the route out of those stupid BFFs so we can win!'

'But if we suddenly show up, they'll know we've been following them!' Kate said.

'From the sound of that screaming, I don't think they'll be too bothered about that now, do you?' Philly said. 'They'll be so desperate for our help, I bet they won't even notice.'

'Why would they tell us which way to go?' Lucinda asked, genuinely intrigued as to what Philly was planning.

'Because we're going to be as nice as pie and tell them we're going to get help. That way they'll tell us the quickest way to camp,' Philly said.

'Oooh, you are wicked, Phil,' Kate said, jumping up and down with excitement. 'We're gonna win this expedition!'

''Course we are!' Philly said with a sly grin. 'Now move!'

'Hold on a sec. What about the emergency location alarm?' Kate said suddenly. 'Surely they'll have already activated that to call for help? And if they have, they won't need our help, so we'll have nothing to trade!'

'What are you saying – that we should get going now and find a way to cross this river?' Philly said.

'Why not? There has to be a way or they wouldn't have come all the way up here. Let's leave them to it. I can't face the sight of blood anyway,' Kate said.

Lucinda rolled her eyes. *Think quickly!* she thought to herself. Even though she didn't know the exact plan, she knew Maria well enough that there would be a way of crossing that river. She couldn't risk Team Dynamo finding it on their own.

'We need to get those L'Etoile girls to stay put. I know them,' Lucinda said. 'They're just as likely to leave the injured girl behind and make a break for the finishing line. They'll have a plan to cross this river. They always have a plan! We need to make them think we're getting help so they don't go anywhere.'

'Why, Lucinda . . . I knew you'd be good for something one of these days.' Philly said. 'OK, we go!'

Molly was still in the middle of an Oscar-worthy performance. She played *agony* like no one played agony.

'Hi!' Philly shouted. 'Need some help over here?'

'Oh, thank goodness!' Maria said, running towards Philly. 'The tree fell just as we were passing. We're all fine, but Molly's in real trouble.'

Philly was horrified to see Molly sticking out from under the most enormous tree.

'Have you tried to lift it?' Kate said, genuinely shocked. It was hard not to be.

'It's too heavy . . . maybe if we all tried . . .' Maria said, but Philly cut her off.

'Might do more damage. You don't know what's been broken,' Philly said.

'Have you sounded your location alarm?' Lucinda said, appearing from behind the rest of Team Dynamo.

'We tried but the battery must have gone or something!' Maria said, giving Lucinda a wink when the others weren't looking.

'Have you guys got yours?' Sally asked.

Philly shot Kate a death stare.

'I'll just have a look,' Kate said, rummaging around in her rucksack. 'Oh, my gosh, it's gone! We must have dropped it when we pulled out the lunch earlier.

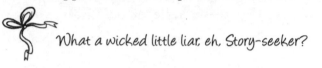

What a wicked little liar, eh, Story-seeker?

'Oh no!' Honey said. Then tears appeared from nowhere, streaming down her cheeks. 'What are we going to do? If we don't get an ambulance here soon, I'm afraid for Molly's life.'

Molly looked up at Honey in astonishment. That was one excellent piece of acting.

'Honey's right. Molly's breathing is getting shallower and she's not screaming as much,' Pippa said.

Molly let out another ear piercing squeal of pain.

'We'll go!' Philly announced.

'Yes, we'll sprint to that finishing line if we have to . . .' Kate said, and then edited her meaning. 'To dispatch the medics, I mean.'

'What way were you planning on going?' Philly said. 'Your way might be quicker than ours and time is of the essence, right?'

'Erm,' Maria said, pretending to be reluctant to share their route.

'Just give it to her!' Sally snapped. 'This is for your sister!'

'I know, I know!' Maria said. 'It's just . . .'

'Just what?' Honey snapped, pretending to be just as angry as Sally.

'It's just . . . I think we screwed up!' Maria said, before looking directly at Philly. 'We've hit a dead end. I thought there was a way to cross here, but it turns out I was wrong. Danya and I have already scouted the area and it's just river-bank. Which way were you going to go? Probably best to follow your original route.'

This question clearly flummoxed Philly, who went bright red in the face and started to pace angrily. 'So you have no quick route across this river?' she spat.

'No!' Maria said angrily, as Molly began to pant as though she were gasping for air. 'Look, you guys just go on. Half of us will stay with Molly and the rest will go for help – which is what we should have done twenty minutes ago.'

'Back down the mountain?' Pippa said, standing up. 'I'll come with you, Maria.'

'No, we'll go. We'll go now. We'll leave all our

equipment with you, though, so we can move quicker. Then you can put it all in the emergency vehicle when it comes to get you . . . OK?' Philly said.

That sly old fox, Maria thought. 'Sure,' she lied. The only way their stuff was getting off that mountain was if Team Dynamo came back for it later!

'It hurts! It hurts!' Molly cried again. She was getting a bit hoarse from all the exclamations so hoped Team Dynamo would get going soon!

'We're going!' Philly said. 'See you on the other side!'

♡

The BFFs watched as Team Dynamo sprinted down the mountain.

'Is the coast clear?' Molly said, heaving a sigh of relief. 'I need to get up. My leg actually feels as if it's broken it's been twisted around for so long!'

'Sorry, Molly!' Maria said, as the girls lifted the log enough for Molly to slide out. 'What a show. Well done. You were brilliant!'

'Can you believe they ditched us with all their stuff like that?' Honey said. 'What on earth are we going to do with it? We can't carry theirs and ours.'

'Of course we can't. We'll just leave it. They'll have

to come back and get it later. It will serve them right,' Danya said.

'OK, guys. Now for the moment of truth! Time to find the *Table Vert* and see if we're right!' Maria said.

'I'm so excited!' Pippa said. 'Sally, can I have a sip of your water? I used all mine up giving Molly life-saving gulps earlier.'

'Yes, you did!' Molly said. 'And I want to be grateful, but I've been so careful not to have too much to drink since embarking on this flipping expedition so I don't need the loo and now I'm desperate. This shortcut had better be quick, Mimi!'

'Let's go. Where's Sally gone now?' Pippa said suddenly.

'Where is she?' Danya said. 'SA-LLY!'

'I wish she'd hurry up! We need to get moving, quickly!' Maria said.

Team BFF sat around for a full ten minutes, before hearing twigs snapping underfoot down the hill.

'Sally!' Pippa exclaimed. 'Where on earth have you—' but she stopped when she saw the panic on Sally's face.

'Guys . . . you have to come quick!' she panted. 'Dump your stuff and follow me!'

'What is it?' Maria demanded, running alongside Sally towards the river.

'It's Lucinda. She . . . she's stuck! And she can't swim!' Sally spluttered.

'What do you mean she can't swim?' Danya said. 'Why would she be swimming?'

'They didn't!' Maria shouted. 'You're not going to tell me they're crossing the river!!'

'They tried to!' Sally said, pointing.

'Is that . . .?' Molly said. 'Oh, my life! Lucinda!'

And there was Lucinda gripping to the branch of a tree in the icy water.

They clambered down the riverbank to get as close as possible to Lucinda, who was flailing around like a fish on a hook.

'Lucinda!' Sally called. 'We're coming to get you!'

'We are?' Pippa said. 'But we can't get close enough. That branch looks like it's going to snap just with Lucinda's weight hanging off it. There's no way we can leverage it to pull her back in.'

'Maria! Please! Do something!' Sally pleaded with Maria, who was racking her brains for something brilliant, but grappling with the problem of having no equipment.

'We need rope!' Maria said, exasperated. 'We can't

do anything without some rope. Does anyone have any in their rucksacks?'

Everyone shook their heads.

'We've got to do something, quickly! She's not moving as much as she was. That water is freezing in there!' Sally wailed.

'Pippa! The bandage!' Molly exclaimed suddenly. 'What did you do with it after you strapped up my knee?'

Pippa patted her jacket pocket. She'd only just finished bandaging Molly when Sally came running through the trees, so the roll of white bandage was still there.

'It's here! I hadn't got around to putting it back yet. Will this do, Maria?' Pippa said, and with a flick of her hand, rolled out an enormous length of white bandage.

'I can't believe it! That's perfect!' Maria said, taking off her boot.

'What are you doing, Maria?' Honey said in alarm. 'Your feet are going to freeze if you go paddling in that water.'

'I've no intention of going into the water. I just need something heavy to tie onto the end of this bandage so we can throw it to Lucinda,' Maria said.

'It will be too flimsy to throw otherwise and will never reach her.'

'What if you knock Lucinda out with that boot!' Sally said, getting more panicked by the second.

'Well, we either try this or she lets go of that branch and we lose her for ever!' Maria said.

'You should throw it, Dan,' Honey said. 'You're always goal shooter and rarely miss in netball.'

'This is hardly the same, Honey!' Danya said. None of the girls were keen to take responsibility for knocking Lucinda out.

'I'll go back to our stuff and bring everything dry and warm we have!' Pippa said, before disappearing with Molly.

'Please, Dan. It's now or never!' Maria said, her eyes beseeching her best friend. 'You can do this.'

Danya grabbed the booted end of the bandage and called to Lucinda. 'Lucinda. You've got to catch this . . .'

Lucinda was quiet. Hanging onto the branch as the icy cold water rushed past her ears. She could see the L'Etoile girls on the bank waving at her, but couldn't hear what they were saying. She was freezing. She couldn't feel her legs. What was Danya doing? She was waving something at her. Now she was throwing

♥ 140 ♥

it. Oh, right . . . they wanted her to catch something. What was that? Was that a boot? A boot on a rope? Would that work? Would it be long enough to reach her? It would have to be!

Lucinda managed to let go of the twig with one hand long enough to give a thumbs-up.

'She understands!' Danya said. 'Right, here goes.'

Danya squinted, just as she did on the netball court, and with her target locked on, launched Maria's boot with all her might, while Maria and Honey held on to the end of the bandage.

There was an almighty thud and a splash. Danya thought she might be sick. She'd closed her eyes as soon as the boot had left her, not wanting to watch in case she hit Lucinda in the face.

'You did it, Dan!' Maria shouted. 'She's got it, look! Now, PULL!'

Danya immediately grabbed the end of the bandage and heaved with Maria and Sally. But the added weight of trying to drag Lucinda against the flow, along with the natural stretch in the bandage, was making it almost impossible to pull her in.

'Don't let go, Lucinda!' Maria screamed, only too aware that her own hands were sweating and starting to slip.

'We need the others!' Sally said. 'Where *are* they?'

On cue, Molly and Pippa appeared on the bank with bundles of clothes, which they threw to the ground and clambered down to the girls.

'PULL!' Sally shrieked as they all grabbed hold of the bandage.

Little by little, they pulled Lucinda out of the water and dragged her up the riverbank.

'Here!' Honey cried, having tipped out Wolf Gornall's emergency brown bag. She passed the girls a silver foil sheet – the sort of thing you use to keep warm after a marathon so your temperature doesn't drop.

'And these!' Maria said, spotting some gel hand warmers on the ground, which heated up when you squeezed them.

Sally set about rubbing Lucinda dry and throwing as many layers of clothes around her as possible.

'What were you thinking?' she snapped at her old companion. 'It was a good job I followed you!'

'You followed her?' Maria said to Sally in amazement. That hadn't been part of the plan.

'Yes, I just got a really bad feeling after the Lakewood girls left. I couldn't stop myself!' Sally said. 'And I was right!'

Lucinda could barely feel her body, but somehow the warmth of friendship around her seemed to bring her strength.

'I didn't see where the others went,' Sally continued. 'I caught up in time to hear you calling for help and couldn't believe my eyes when I saw you clinging to that branch!'

'Philly made me go first . . .' Lucinda said, her teeth chattering uncontrollably. 'To test it out! She said it couldn't be that deep or you guys wouldn't have brought us all the way up here. She was convinced you just didn't want to give up your game plan!'

'But I don't get it! Why didn't one of them stay with you while the others ran to camp or came back to us for help?' Pippa said. 'You weren't going to be able to hang onto that branch for long!'

'I . . . I don't know,' Lucinda sobbed as she felt her toes start to come back to life. 'Philly just ordered them on and they went.'

'Oh, I can't bear it. It's too awful for words!' Molly exclaimed.

'Lucinda, do you think you can stand up?' Sally said softly. 'You need to get out of these wet things or you'll never get warm.'

'Yes,' Lucinda said, smiling at her friend. 'I'm so sorry, Sally. For everything I put you through.'

'There's plenty of time for that,' Sally said. 'But thank you for saying it.'

'Fancy getting a bit of revenge and kitting yourself out in some of Miss Malby's stuff?' Pippa said, holding up a navy cashmere sweater.

'Oh, yes,' Molly said, waving half a dozen luxury items in the air. 'We raided her bag first as it was the heaviest. I've never seen so much cashmere! She's even got a spare pair of brand new boots in there. I just hope they'll fit you.'

'No wonder I nearly collapsed if that's what I've been carrying around for her!' Lucinda said.

'Don't suppose she's got two spare pairs and some cashmere socks has she?' Maria said, looking down at her sodden hero of a boot.

'No, but I have!' Molly said with a grin, showing Maria a pair of sparkling new hiking boots.

''Course you have!' Maria exclaimed, giving her sister a big hug. 'When have you ever not had three outfit changes in your bag – just in case?!'

'Lucky for you, Mimi. Lucky for you!' Molly said.

'Come on. Let's get to that camp. I reckon we still might have a shot at this. It'll take them at least an hour to get to the village road, and another hour to climb back up the other side of the river, so if *Table Vert* is what we think it is, we're still in with a chance,' Maria said, revving up the group.

'Lucinda, how are you feeling? Are you able to walk?' Molly said.

'Here, eat this!' Danya said, passing her a chocolate bar. 'Nothing like a hit of chocolate to boost your energy reserves.'

'You're lucky she hasn't given you the dehydrated insects!' Maria grinned.

'Thank you,' Lucinda said, slightly confused by the insect comment. 'All of you. I'll be fine in a minute. I just haven't really eaten or slept properly since we got to France – and then spending all that time in that freezing water, I think my body's gone into shock.'

'I bet it has,' Molly said. 'Guys, can you manage to carry mine and Sally's things between you? It's just this last bit. Then Lucinda can put an arm around each of our shoulders as a crutch.'

'Are you sure?' Lucinda said, her lips beginning to lose their blue colour.

'One hundred per cent!' Danya said, as she loaded herself up with the extra baggage. 'It's nice to meet you, by the way. I'm Danya, and that's my sister, Honey.'

Lucinda smiled. 'I'm Lucinda. Lovely to meet you too.'

And so it was, Story-seeker, that after years of fighting each other tooth and nail, all was forgiven and for the first time ever, Marciano, Fitzfoster, Burrows, Sudbury and Sawyer were all on the same team!

★ ★ ★

16

Table Vert

*I*t took Team BFF+1 a lot longer than Maria had anticipated to climb the steep track to *Table Vert*. Partly due to the fact that they were all carrying heavier loads, and partly because they had to go at a slower pace for Lucinda. That said, the seven girls were enjoying every minute of reminiscing about the past few years when they'd been arch-enemies.

'The truth is, I envied you!' Lucinda said to Maria.

'You envied me? But you hated me!' Maria said in shock.

'That's true, but it didn't mean I wasn't completely impressed by your genius. Nothing ever fazed you.'

'Really?' Maria said, astounded. 'If I'd have known you were such a fan, you wouldn't have got on my nerves so much!'

'Oh, to have our time again,' Lucinda said thoughtfully.

'Look!' Danya breathed. '*Table Vert*! The green shelf!'

Even Lucinda managed to pick up the pace a bit, keen to see this natural stone shelf she'd been told so much about.

'Oh, Mimi, you're so clever. You did it! It's exactly as you described,' Molly said.

Maria glowed with pride. She loved it when a plan came together. It had been a risk, but one worth taking. If hers and Danya's calculations were right, the finish line was about a mile the other side of the river.

'Isn't it breath-taking?' Pippa said, as she stared at the enormous slabs of green rock protruding above the river like a great stone runway.

'Shall we?' Maria said.

'After you!' Danya answered excitedly.

'Just be careful. *Table Vert* gets its name because it's covered with green algae which is bound to be like an ice rink,' Maria warned.

There wasn't a factoid she didn't know,
was there, Story-seeker?

Team BFF + 1 crossed the river in silence, completely focused on not falling in, and no one was quieter than Lucinda. She'd had quite enough of fast flowing icy water for one day.

'We did it! Wasn't that amazing?' Danya said. 'Let's have a quick selfie with *Table Vert* in the background so we can show everyone later. They're not going to believe it!'

'Good idea! Might even email it to Philly over the Christmas holidays! That will be galling – to know this crossing was here all the time!' Lucinda said.

'Be my guest!' Danya said. 'Just make sure we have your email and I'll send it to you.'

'Right, Team BFF! Let's win this thing!' Maria announced.

'Hands!' Sally shouted, before grabbing Lucinda's hand and the others all piled on top.

'Whooooop!' they called out and off they went.

Team BFF, we're on our way
Hiking is our favourite play

Preparation is a must
We're Team BFF, so eat our dust!

17

Crossing The Finish Line

'You seem to be walking a bit easier, Lucinda,' Sally said, noticing how Lucinda didn't seem to be leaning on her quite so heavily.

'I know. I can actually feel my legs to put one foot in front of the other. They were so cold when we started, I wasn't even sure I could stand up, let alone walk to the finish line! I've no idea how I crossed that river without falling back in!' Lucinda admitted.

'Then we shouldn't have made you try! I wish you'd said how bad it was,' Molly exclaimed.

'Not at all. If anything it's done me good getting the blood pumping around my system again. I might even be able to manage on my own now,' Lucinda said, pulling away, only to wobble as she let go.

'Don't run before you can walk!' Sally warned with a smile.

'Shhhhh! Guys! Can you hear that?' Pippa said suddenly. She always did have the best hearing of all of them. It must have been why she had such excellent pitch when singing!

'I don't hear anything,' Molly said. 'Just that low humming noise.'

'Exactly!' Maria said, picking up the pace. 'It's the camp generators!! Girls, we're so close!'

'I wonder if anyone's made it before us?' Danya said eagerly.

'Only one way to find out,' Pippa said. 'I reckon we could move a bit quicker, guys. Lucinda?'

'We've got you,' Sally reassured her.

'Then yes!' Lucinda said.

And with that, Team BFF + 1 sped up.

'There's the finish line! I can see the Chateau Pierre banner!' Honey cried. 'Come on, girls! We're so nearly there!'

Maria, Danya, Pippa and Honey made a mad dash for it, to a multitude of cheers as they passed under the *Grande Expedition* banner.

'And here's the first team through the post . . .' came Madame Renard's voice over the loudspeaker. 'And who is it? Yes, it looks like . . . Team BFF from L'Etoile!'

Everyone clapped and cheered as they watched the four girls hug each other.

'But hold on . . . what's that, three L'Etoile stragglers?' Madame Renard said. 'Come on, girls. The rules state that the entire team has to make it over the finishing line to complete the course.'

'COME ON, MOLL!' Maria shouted! 'WE'VE DONE IT! WE'VE REALLY DONE . . .' Then she stopped short, distracted by another group of girls hurtling out of nowhere towards them.

'Philly!' Danya gasped.

'NOOOOOOOO!' Pippa shouted. 'This isn't fair! SA-LLY, COME ON!!'

But it was too late. Despite Molly, Sally and Lucinda only being about ten paces away, they couldn't beat the sprinting Dynamos, especially given how light they were, having dumped all their equipment up the mountain.

'And Team Dynamo have taken it!' Madame Renard cried. '*Felicitations, les filles!* This is closest-run expedition I think we've ever had!'

'I'm so sorry!' Molly said breathlessly, as she crossed the finish line with Sally, leaving Lucinda to cross the line a couple of paces behind under her own steam.

'No, it's my fault,' Lucinda said, joining them. 'If you hadn't stopped to rescue me and then had to practically carry me all the way back here, you'd have won with hours to spare!' Tears pricked her eyes. She couldn't bear to see Philly and the Dynamos jumping up and down with excitement.

'Don't be crazy!' Sally said. 'Do you honestly think we'd have wanted to win if it had meant leaving you to drown?'

'But it's not fair! And surely there must be something in the rules about ditching your equipment along the way!' Lucinda said, calling on every ounce of the cunning she'd buried long ago.

'It doesn't matter, Lucinda, honestly,' Pippa said. 'At least we're all in one piece and that's what counts.'

'And at least you managed to stand on your own two feet and cross that finish line as Lucinda Marciano – not being held up by us, or downtrodden by Team Dynamo,' Sally said.

'Sally Sudbury. You are a genius!' Maria said, the biggest grin beginning to cross her face.

'I am?' Sally said in surprise. 'Why?'

'What is it, Maria?' Danya said. She knew that look on her friend's face and it wasn't the look of a loser!

'You'll see!' Maria continued, before she was interrupted by a very excited Miss Ward and Miss Denham, who came rushing over to congratulate their girls.

'Oh, L'Etoilettes! We're so very proud of you! Second place! You wait until we tell Madame Ruby. She will be over the moon!' Miss Denham said.

'Actually, Miss Denham,' Maria said. 'There's a bit of a problem.'

'A problem?' Miss Ward said. 'Oh, Maria. Please don't tell me you've been up to anything untoward. I couldn't bear for you to lose your place as silver medalists.'

'We get medals?!' Molly and Honey said together, immediately thinking how cool an accessory that would be to flaunt about for the rest of the term.

'I'm afraid we might indeed lose our silver medals,' Maria said, grinning from ear to ear. 'You remember Lucinda Marciano, don't you?'

The two form tutors gasped. They had been so busy being proud of Team BFF they hadn't noticed their newfound seventh member. Miss Ward had been one of the staff members around the time of Lucinda's fake haunting of L'Etoile who'd been particularly freaked out by the whole thing, so to see Lucinda's face again unexpectedly was quite a shock.

'Errr. Yes. Miss Marciano. Hello . . . But I don't understand . . . do I?' Miss Ward stammered.

'Sorry, I'm not explaining this very well, am I?' Maria said. She took a deep breath. 'To give you the short version, Lucinda Marciano was abandoned by her Lakewood High team mates when she fell into a river, because they couldn't afford the *time* to rescue her. Luckily, we, Team BFF, saved Lucinda from drowning and assisted her back to camp, even though it meant us having to slow down and sacrifice our place in the competition.'

Miss Ward and Miss Denham's faces were a picture. Their girls were heroines!

'It's true,' Lucinda said softly. 'They saved my life!'

'What an ordeal!' Miss Denham said. 'What heroics! Are you feeling all right, Lucinda?'

'I'm much better now, thanks to the girls,' Lucinda said.

Miss Ward looked at Miss Denham in astonishment. This couldn't be the same girl. The same girl who'd terrorised the school and made everyone's life a misery, staff and students alike.

Miss Ward took a breath. 'Aside from . . . well, pretty much everything, one thing I don't understand is why you said you're going to lose your second place medals. If anything, you should be getting a trophy for your exceptional bravery here today.'

'I just don't think we deserve silver,' Maria said, still grinning like a Cheshire cat.

'You don't?' Miss Ward said, baffled.

'No, I don't. When Madame Renard announced our arrival in first place, we were quickly demoted to second place as Sally and Molly weren't with us when we crossed the finish line, because they were helping Lucinda. It was at this point, where we were waiting for Sally and Molly, that Team Dynamo appeared out of nowhere and crossed just in front of them to take first place.' Maria paused to see if the penny had dropped with anyone else.

'Maria, you genius!!' Danya squealed, giving Maria a squeeze. 'Madame Renard said herself that the entire team had to cross the finish line in order for it to count. We were given second place as Molly and Sally weren't with us. But here's the thing: Team Dynamo weren't complete when they crossed either—' Danya said.

'Because of me!' Lucinda interrupted, her face

flushing with colour. 'Team Dynamo weren't complete because of me! They could never have won – even if they'd crossed an hour earlier than you guys because they'd ditched me on the mountain.'

'Exactly!' Maria said happily.

'But you guys came through together!' Pippa said, looking at Sally, Molly and Lucinda. 'Who's to say whether Lucinda crossed first, meaning her team win or if you girls crossed first meaning we win?'

'That's easy!' Lucinda said. 'I asked the girls to let me walk the last few steps on my own, which they did, and they ran on ahead!'

'So we win gold?' Pippa asked, eyes flashing.

'Oh, my goodness, we won!!' Honey exclaimed.

'I'll just be a moment,' Miss Denham said, as she skipped over to where Madame Renard was still announcing the groups crossing the finishing line.

'*Excusez-moi!* Everyone. It has come to my attention that the current winners, Team Dynamo from Lakewood High, were a girl down when they crossed the finish line. There will be an enquiry into exactly what has taken place here today within the ranks of Team Dynamo, but for the moment, I can announce that Team BFF of L'Etoile, School for Stars, are the winners of *La Grande Expedition* . . . and

Team Dynamo are disqualified!'

'HURRAH!!' cheered Team BFF+1.

'We did it! We really did it! My hero!' Molly said to Maria.

'You're all heroes!' Lucinda said. 'You deserve this victory.'

'Hey! Danya! Girls! Congratulations!' Belle said, pushing her way through to Team BFF. 'Who'd have thought, eh? With Team Dynamo being disqualified...'

'We got silver!' Ellie said, utterly ecstatic.

'No way! That's great. L'Etoile took first and second place. I can't believe it!' Sally said.

'Wait until Old Ruby hears about this one! She'll be over the moon!' Pippa said. 'And what about Team Mars and Team Swift. Anyone seen them yet?'

'Not yet,' Ellie said.

Suddenly a scuffle broke out as a bright red, irate Philly Malby burst through the hoards of excited girls.

'*Hollywood*, you wait! You cheating liar!' she spat. 'And as for you, you stupid School for Stars girls... this is not over!'

'Actually, Miss Malby,' Madame Renard boomed, appearing from nowhere. 'You are absolutely correct. This is far from over. You and your team's behaviour on that mountain today was wicked. How dare you abandon anyone in such serious circumstances, circumstances which you yourself created, by all accounts?'

Philly, and indeed everyone, stood in stunned silence.

'Ah, Mrs Cauldwell,' Madame Renard said, on seeing a short, rotund woman entering the group. 'My staff have been looking for you. Chateau Pierre holds you entirely accountable for the actions of your Lakewood students today and you may be assured that Lakewood High School will never again be welcomed back to this programme.'

Mrs Cauldwell was red with embarrassment.

'I . . . I'm not sure exactly what has transpired here, but I can only apologise on behalf of these students and assure you that serious steps will be taken to reprimand any inappropriate behaviour,' Mrs Caldwell said.

'Blimey. Go, Madame Fox!' Maria whispered to Danya, as Philly and co were escorted away from the celebrations.

'I'm sorry to say, ladies, that you will have to give statements. Chateau Pierre takes student safety issues very, very seriously indeed,' Madame Renard said as she turned back to Lucinda and the others.

'That will be fine,' Miss Denham said. 'Just one more

thing, Madame Renard. Mrs Cauldwell does seem to have forgotten that Lucinda here is a Lakewood student, and she has, once again, been left behind. I have to say, however, that I would be nervous to let her return with her peers.'

'Oh, please, no!' Lucinda said. The thought of having to travel home with a raging Philly filled her with dread.

'I would agree, Miss Denham,' Madame Renard said, gravely, before looking at Lucinda. 'Far be it for me to advise you, Lucinda, but if you felt you wanted to use the phone in my office back at the chateau, to speak with your parents and explain your reasons for wanting to travel home independently, I would be happy to make alternative arrangements for you.'

Lucinda burst into tears of relief.

'She could travel back with us, couldn't she?' Sally said, her eyes pleading with Miss Ward and Miss Denham.

The two teachers looked at one another.

'I don't see why not. But, Lucinda, you must make arrangements to be met at London Heathrow airport and taken home. Is that understood?' Miss Denham said.

'Thank you. Oh, thank you,' Lucinda said.

She couldn't wait to get back to Los Angeles. She'd had enough of English schools and freezing temperatures. It was time to reinvent herself at home, the way she'd done with the L'Etoile girls today, and start living a happy life. It was going to be a long and bumpy road, given her past reputation, but if Maria's newfound acceptance of her had taught her something, it was that *anything* is possible!

'Come on then, girls. It's time to collect your medals!' Madame Renard said.

'Yesssssss!' they whispered and marched hand in hand to the podium to take their positions, alongside Belle's Beagles in second place and a team from Claremont High School in third.

It truly was a proud moment in all the girls' lives, made even more magical by sharing it with each other.

♡ ♥ ♡

18

Home At Last

'Are you sure you're going to be all right?' Sally whispered as she gave Lucinda a hug goodbye in the arrivals hall at Heathrow airport.

'More than ever.' Lucinda smiled, her face softened with happiness. 'Look – Elodie's here to take me back to LA . . . Elodie! Hi! Over here . . .'

'Miss Denham. Thanks so much for bringing me back with you and please make sure you give Madame Ruby and Mrs Fuller my letters. I need them to believe how sorry I am, for everything,' Lucinda said, turning to her old teachers.

'We will, Lucinda. An excellent lesson has been learned here this weekend and we wish you all the very best for your new life in LA,' Miss Denham said.

Having made her peace with as many of the fourth-years as possible on the way back to England, Lucinda was on Cloud Nine. Never in her wildest dreams did she imagine a person could feel like this.

'Good luck, Lucifette,' Maria said with a wink. 'Stay in touch.'

'Ooooh, yes! Stay in touch. Might even see you in LA when I'm next over,' Molly said.

'Might even bump into you at a movie audition!' Lucinda said. 'But if that's the case, I'll be walking straight back out of the door. I've no chance of beating your acting skills . . . not with that contortionist leg of yours!'

'Ha! You know it!' Molly grinned.

'See you, my friend,' Sally said.

'Take care of yourself, Sally Sudbury! And send my love to your mum. Her toad-in-the-hole was always the best!' Lucinda said.

'By-eeeee!' everyone called as Lucinda disappeared up the escalator, on her way back to her Hollywood home.

'I know I've had about twenty baths since we got back from France, but after that weekend without hot water, I don't think I'll ever take them for granted again!' Molly said, slumping on her bed at Garland, a wet towel twirled around her head like a turban.

'It's not having to go around carrying twice your body weight in rucksack any more that I love!' Honey said. 'I don't even mind running up that hill behind the lake in PE. Anything's a doddle after Parc du Mercantour!'

'How proud was Madame Ruby this morning in assembly? I still can't get over the fact that a) we won our expedition weekend, and b) we won with Lucifette!' Maria said.

'I know. The whole school's talking about it!' Danya said. 'Lucinda must have been a real piece of work when she was a student here. I even heard a couple of sixth-formers saying they didn't believe a leopard could change that many bad spots!'

'See, miracles can happen!' Pippa said.

'And they do all the time at L'Etoile, it seems!' Sally said happily.

'What on earth are those?' Molly said, suddenly spotting three large body-shaped bags laid on Pippa's bed.

'Oh, yes! Miss Coates just brought those in for you, Molly!' Pippa said, throwing her toothbrush back in the pot.

'Really?' Molly said, jumping up from her bed and grabbing the large envelope taped to the front.

'Dear Molly,' she read.

'You're probably already sorted for the première, but these came in for you, just in case you're undecided! Don't worry about returning any of them. They're gifts from the designers – all hoping you'll pick theirs to wear on the big night! Can't wait to see your dazzling smile on the red carpet.

Love, Tara Jones.'

'Wow!' Honey said.

'Who's Tara Jones?' Maria said.

'She was Head of Wardrobe on the Warner Brothers movie,' Molly breathed, too excited to unzip the first bag.

'And she's sent you some outfits for the première! OMG!' Honey squealed with delight.

'What are you waiting for?' Pippa said.

'Yes! Let's take a look!' Sally said.

Molly unzipped the first bag to reveal a flash of lavender satin.

'I can't do it! Let me just savour this for a second,' she said, her hand cupping her mouth. 'Designers from all over the world have sent me, Molly Fitzfoster, their best clothes to wear! Can you believe it?'

'I can, and you deserve it, Moll,' Maria said, putting her arm around Molly's shoulders. 'This is your time to shine. Now try them on!'

Molly was in tears as she examined dress after dress. The most beautiful collection she'd ever seen and each one perfect in a different way. These would keep her going for the next ten years, never mind one première.

'It's got to be that one!' Honey squealed as Molly pulled out the last dress. A crimson velvet fifties-style dress with a wide sequin sash tied into an enormous bow at the back.

'OOOOOOOoooooh!' Molly cried as she danced around with it against her. 'I agree. It's . . . it's perfect.'

'Try it on immediately!' Pippa instructed, and within thirty seconds, Molly was standing there in all her glory.

'Oh, Molly. You look like a Christmas doll!' Sally said.

'It's exquisite – the detail, the colour, the shape – it's like it's been made to fit your measurements exactly!' Honey said.

'Well, they do have my measurements, so it probably was!' Molly said, beaming at her reflection in the mirror.

'And it's the perfect colour for a Christmas première!' Danya said, ever the practical one.

'And you know what this means?' Molly said with a grin.

'What?' the others said.

'That you get your pick of the other nine!' Molly exclaimed.

'We can't!' Pippa said, eyeing up the sky-blue tulle number.

'No, we couldn't possibly!' Sally said, loving a long yellow chiffon maxi-dress with matching shrug.

'Oh, but we could!' Honey said, all over a bejewelled emerald dress.

'Yes, you could!' Molly said. 'Oh my, how are we ever going to get to sleep now!'

'Yes . . . I was just thinking that! Tomorrow's a big day for us. We've got to hit the ground running with our fourth-year choir rehearsals or we'll never be ready in time for the end of term Christmas concert,' Maria said thoughtfully.

'How's the arrangement going, Pips?' Sally said.

'We're nearly there. Thank goodness Mrs Fuller built in those extra music sessions for me to meet with Lara and the rest of the band, or I'd be in a complete spin tonight!' Pippa answered.

'I know, you lucky things – while we've been out freezing our bottoms off in PE, you girls have been warm and cosy in the Mozart Rooms making sweet music!' Molly exclaimed.

'I think you're going to love it when we put it all together tomorrow,' Pippa said. 'At least I *hope* you will!'

'I know we will!' Danya, the One Direction superfan said. 'Oh, and BTW, any gossip on whether the boys are going to put in a surprise appearance at the concert? You know, as a special favour to the songwriter?!'

'Dan-ya!' Maria shouted. 'Will you give it up? Honestly, you're insane!'

'Bed! Now!' Honey said, taking charge of her deluded sister. 'And leave your laptop in here. I'm not having another night of listening to your earphones hissing out One Direction tunes in the dark.'

'OK, OK!' Danya said.

'Night, Team BFF!' Maria said.

'Night!'

19

Christmas Countdown

There wasn't a sound in the Kodak Hall as the house lights went down after the final Christmas reading for the headlining act to perform. The fourth-years were huddled together in their finery, waiting for the spotlights to go up and to sing their hearts out. Following a meeting with Fashion Faye about costumes, Mrs Fuller had agreed that the girls could wear evening gowns instead of the more traditional choir capes and they all looked splendid. Only Molly had saved her red dress for the première happening the following evening. Team BFF were all sporting the dresses she'd lent them. They could afford to be seen in the same outfit two days in a row. The world's press weren't going to be on them!

As the percussion commenced with the sound of distant sleigh-bells, Pippa gripped Danya's hand.

'You ready for this?' she whispered.

'Absolutely! I knew it by heart before we even started rehearsals!' Danya said.

'No, not that . . . this!' Pippa said, before pointing to where a spotlight had fallen on a platform at the side of the stage.

'Oh . . . my . . . god!' Danya breathed, as four faces appeared in the light. Four fabulous, beautiful faces. Four male faces.

A scream went up from everyone in the hall.

'One Direction!'

'They're here! They're really here!'

'Am I dreaming?'

'Arrrrrrrggggggghhhhhhhhhhh!'

'Surprise!' Pippa shouted above the din as a million flash bulbs went off.

OK! Magazine were in a frenzy at the front. Not even they had been let into Pippa and Mrs Fuller's secret, who with the help of Mr Fuller, had managed to co-ordinate this little surprise visit to L'Etoile. With the country's top gossip magazine being present, it was excellent promo for everyone involved.

The fourth-years sung their hearts out, accompanying the boys, although it would be true to say most of them forgot the lyrics at some point, but who could blame them? It wasn't every day you were in the company of superstars!

Christmas-time for you and for me
Christmas-time for family
And if you don't know where to go
Meet me under the mistletoe

When the song finished, the room went dark and by the time the lights came back on, the platform stood empty.

'Good evening, ladies and gentlemen!' Madame Ruby said as she swooshed onto the stage, wearing an outfit to rival the Christmas tree she stood next to. 'You could be forgiven for wondering whether that was indeed a dream, but I can assure you that it did just happen . . .'

The room erupted into applause once again.

'Where have they gone, Pips?' Danya asked beseechingly.

'Unfortunately, the boys have another engagement

and are already back on their tour bus, so we are particularly thrilled and honoured that they made this pit-stop en route and want to thank Mr Fuller for using his music industry influence to make this happen. I know I speak for everyone when I say — what a Christmas present that was!'

The girls cheered and stamped their feet in agreement.

'Thank you, too, to *OK!* Magazine, for taking the time to come and commemorate our little school. I can think of no better way to round off my final term here as headmistress. It has been a pleasure working with all the girls and staff at L'Etoile, School for Stars, and I shall dedicate the rest of my days to following your success on the world stage. Merry Christmas, one and all, and good evening,' Madame Ruby said, wiping away a tear.

'Three cheers!' Maria shouted. 'Hip, hip!'

'Hooray!' the room exploded.

'Hip, hip!'

'Hooray!'

'Hip, hip!'

'Hoooo-ray!'

'If I do nothing else in my life I can honestly say I'll die happy, after last night!' Danya said. She'd barely had a wink of sleep since the boys' performance.

'Are you still going on about it, sis?' Honey said, gazing out of the window of the stretch limo that Warner Brothers had sent to take Molly and her plus five to the première.

'Yes, I am! It's like a dream! Weren't they so much taller in real life?' Danya said. 'Like giants of the pop world!'

'Oh, just ignore her! Molly this is your night. How do you feel?' Honey said.

'I don't know,' Molly said, her red lipgloss glistening. 'I'm soooooo nervous!'

'Don't worry. If you do or say something wrong, I'll do one of my classic nose dives and take all the heat away from you!' Sally said, a vision in yellow.

'Mum and Dad have just texted. They're waiting for us at the red carpet entrance,' Maria said. 'Look, they've sent a photo. Don't they look glam?'

'They look OOTW!' Molly grinned.

'Oh my – isn't that . . . yes, it is! It's Ameera! Look – getting out of a limo! She's here for you, Molly!' Sally squealed with delight.

'Wow,' Molly whispered under her breath. It was all coming together.

'You're right, Sal! Good spot! We might have guessed she'd be here. She's over for the football match with us this weekend – of course she'd come early for tonight! What a stroke of luck!' Maria said.

'How long, driver?' Danya said, knocking gently on the privacy window.

'Actually, it's just around this corner. Are you ready, ladies?' the driver asked, as he turned into London's Leicester Square.

'Ready as I'll ever be!' Molly mumbled under her breath. This was it. The moment she had been waiting for. Her very first red carpet event, where she was the star . . . she was who the crowds were waiting to meet.

Maria gripped her hand. 'I'm here,' she said softly.

'I know,' Molly said. 'I love you.'

'Love you too! Now get out of this car and go and meet your fans!'

A burly security guard opened the limo door and stood by as six dazzling ladies climbed out, led by the beautiful Molly.

'Molly, darling. You look a picture! I'm so proud!' her dad whispered in her ear as he hugged her with all his might.

'Thanks, Dad. I'm terrified!' Molly stammered, her red sequin sash glittering in the paparazzi flashes. All around her, people were calling out her name for an autograph or a photo.

'I don't think my legs will move!' she said.

'There might be someone here to give you a hand with that,' Brian Fitzfoster said, nodding over Molly's shoulder.

Molly turned around to see the most beautifully groomed little black dog, waiting patiently with her equally well-turned-out owner.

'Twinkle!' Molly squealed with delight, as her friends watched. 'Mr Hart, what are you doing here?'

'The girls thought you might need a date for your première, and Twinkle insisted!' he said, passing Molly the ruby-encrusted lead. 'They're real rubies, you know . . . courtesy of your dad!'

'No way!' Molly breathed as Twinkle glittered in the light.

'Woof!' Twinkle barked as she started to lead Molly away.

'Oh, thank you, Mr Hart. She's just what I needed!' she said.

Before turning to face the red carpet, she tugged gently at Twinkle to stop.

'I love you so much, girls,' she called, her eyes brimming with tears. 'You're the best friends anyone could ever ask for!'

The girls looked at each other and grabbed each other's hands.

'Ditto!' they shouted. 'BFFS FOREVER!'

'BFFs forever,' Molly whispered back and turned to face her public.